But apparently he'd given her something, too.

If he stopped to think about it, the awesome responsibility of two fragile little lives was enough to make him want to run in the other direction.

But he thought about his mystery woman instead and wondered why she hadn't simply come to him and told him she was pregnant. Or why she hadn't stayed with the babies and waited for him to come home.

He remembered the tenderness of her touch, the gentle whispers in his ear, the generosity of her response to him. He couldn't reconcile those memories to a woman who would abandon her babies to a man who didn't even know her name.

Then, at a thought, he smiled in the dark. She hadn't abandoned them. She was biding her time, for some reason he didn't yet understand.

She would come back. Unless he found her first.

cliff, and sat in the chair facing Digon at. Her eyes were

Dear Reader,

Okay... I'm hooked on babies. As the Jensen-Baker families swell with more and more grandchildren for Ron and me, I'm able to study and adore them while being removed from the responsibility of parenthood.

Julia is our newest addition to the family, a sturdy, bright little bundle who just had her first birthday. I've always thought she was so beautiful, she should have been twins—and a writer's personal life always ends up in her books.

So I began to imagine what would have happened if Julia had been twins born to a woman who was unable at that point in time to provide for them. What would become of them?

Enter the pulse of every romance novel: the hero.

The twins' mother would send them to their father, but who was he? My imagination created three possibilities, and when I couldn't decide among them, the McKeon brothers were born.

Now with three heroines to provide the spark each brother is missing in his life, I leave you to decide why the mother left her babies, and WHO'S THE DADDY? Darrick, the hospital administrator; Dillon, the orthopedist; or Duncan, the actor?

Muriel

Muriel Jensen
Daddy By Destiny

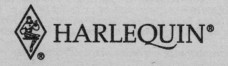

HARLEQUIN®

TORONTO • NEW YORK • LONDON
AMSTERDAM • PARIS • SYDNEY • HAMBURG
STOCKHOLM • ATHENS • TOKYO • MILAN • MADRID
PRAGUE • WARSAW • BUDAPEST • AUCKLAND

To Peggy Hanson,
cohort and confidante

ISBN 0-373-16746-6

DADDY BY DESTINY

Copyright © 1998 by Muriel Jensen.

This edition published by arrangement with Harlequin Books S.A.

® and TM are trademarks of the publisher. Trademarks indicated with ® are registered in the United States Patent and Trademark Office, the Canadian Trade Marks Office and in other countries.

Printed in U.S.A.

Chapter One

Duncan McKeon smiled into the back of the limo at Steven Spielberg. "Thanks for the lift home, Steven," he said. "And I'm flattered by your insistence, but I don't think it's the role for me."

"You're wrong." Spielberg adjusted the bill of his baseball cap, which was emblazoned with the title of his latest film, *King of Camelot.* "Every villain you've ever played was a hero at heart."

They'd been arguing this same point throughout the flight from New York, and in the limo that had picked them up at the Portland, Oregon airport. Duncan had tried repeatedly—and so far unsuccessfully—to convince the director that his film audience was accustomed to seeing him solely as a villain, and that putting him in the role of heroic Arthur Pendragon could jeopardize the project.

"But don't think about it any more until August first," Spielberg said. "Rest, relax, enjoy this time with your family." He pointed out the tinted window at the group of men and women gathered on the lawn. "Looks like they're ready to welcome you." Then he pointed back over his shoulder to the crowd of screaming women that had followed the limo from downtown

Dancer's Beach. "You think you'd get this kind of attention from an audience that couldn't believe in you as a hero? I'll be waiting for your call. Have a good vacation."

Spielberg leaned forward to shake Duncan's hand.

"Thank you." Duncan straightened and closed the door, then watched the long limo drive slowly away, still amazed that he'd spent the last twelve hours in the company of the man who'd made most of the top-grossing films of all time. And even more amazed that he'd been trying to talk his way *out* of starring in the man's next project.

It was very hard to tell Steven Spielberg that he was mistaken.

Duncan was forced to dismiss his thoughts when a middle-aged woman who didn't even reach his shoulder threw her arms around his middle and squeezed. "Oh, Devlin!" she said breathlessly, calling him by the name of the character he'd played in *Gone Before Morning*. "You have to stop *using* people. You need a good woman to set you straight."

"Mother, *please!*" A young woman in shorts and a tank top, peeled the older woman from him. She smiled apologetically at Duncan. "Ignore her, she's menopausal. But would you sign this, please?" She handed him a *People Magazine* with his face on the cover.

"Of course." He took the pen she also handed him and scrawled his name. Women pressed closer, waving copies of the magazine, blank paper, napkins, articles of clothing he didn't want to examine too closely.

He was acutely exhausted after six weeks of six-teen-hour days on the set in a miserably uncomfortable location in central Africa, but he knew that he owed his career and every luxury he'd acquired because of it to fans like these all over the world. And he had to admit to himself that he'd be a poor second fiddle right now if they knew who had been in the limo that just drove away.

But Duncan had been the one who'd had to stop for aspirin at the drugstore in town and been recognized by a pair of teenage girls studying a case of costume jewelry.

By the time he'd gotten back to the limo, he'd picked up a crowd.

He signed the offerings of those closest to him, then blew a kiss intended to encompass the crowd. "Thank you, ladies," he said. "I love you, too. But I'm on vacation for the next few weeks."

They shrieked delightedly in response, those at the back trying to press forward.

He was trying hard not to step on the colorful high-tops of a group of young girls who'd obviously left cheerleader practice to follow him, when he felt a strong tug on both his arms. He looked up to see that his brothers had come to his rescue. Dillon held his left arm; Darrick, his right.

"Let him through, ladies," Darrick said, grinning at the crowd. "He's not half as interesting as he seems."

There was a wave of giggles as the crowd now surged around his rescuers.

"Yeah," Dillon added, gently clearing the girls from his path. "*And* he wears boxers. With cartoon characters. I mean, really."

One of the cheerleaders, a leggy little blonde with enormous eyes, turned her attention from Duncan to Dillon.

"What do *you* wear?" she asked suggestively.

Dillon opened his mouth to answer but was interrupted by a squeal from an older woman in the rear of the crowd. "They're as hunky as he is! Form a wedge, ladies. We're fighting our way through!"

"Hold it!" That order was followed by a sudden intrusion into the fray by Harper Harriman, a young woman Duncan had thought was out of his brother Dillon's life forever. She stepped between the women, and Duncan and his brothers.

"He may belong to you on the screen," she said, shooing the crowd back. "But on his vacation, he belongs to his family. Give him a break, ladies. Even hunks need their rest."

Duncan watched in amazement as the crowd backed away under her forceful stare. Darrick and Dillon took advantage of the moment and swept him onto the sidewalk. The family closed ranks around him to protect his retreat down the driveway.

He was ushered into the backyard littered with lawn chairs and a barbecue filled with dying coals. Plates, cups, napkins, purses, sweaters and hats were strewn everywhere. He turned to laugh with his brothers and realized that though the ladies had dispersed, a veritable crowd was still following him.

It was true that he hadn't been home in almost a year, and out of reach even by phone and e-mail for a good ten weeks. But when he'd left for Africa, he'd had just two parents, two brothers, and a sister. Who were all these people?

He turned in the middle of the yard, and a large circle formed around him, several people deep.

Darrick caught him in a bear hug. "How the hell are you?" he demanded, laughing. "How come you didn't have that kind of babe appeal when we were in school? You'd have saved Dillon and me an awful lot of trouble. We could just have taken what was left over.''

"Because he wasn't a villain then.'' Dillon moved in to embrace him. "He was passing himself off as a nice guy.''

"Only until I discovered there was no money in it.'' Duncan clapped his youngest brother on the back, then held him at arm's length to frown fondly at him.

It still amazed Duncan that his own face had been the one to capture national attention. His brothers were equally photogenic; Darrick and Dillon had the same dark eyes and hair and angular features.

But they were good guys and looked it. Maybe that was the key. People liked to cheer someone else's villainy because they couldn't indulge their own.

"And for your information, I don't wear boxers,'' Duncan said. "And cartoon characters? Please.''

Dillon nodded with feigned penitence. "I know, but the situation was desperate.''

"Oh, *you're* desperate.'' Dorianne, Duncan's only sister and the youngest McKeon, pushed Dillon aside to wrap her arms around Duncan. She had the McKeon hair and eyes, but was small, like their mother.

"Hi,'' Dori said, squeezing him. "It's about time you got home. We were all beginning to wonder if you'd gone bush on us and decided not to come back.''

"And miss brot-and-beer night? Don't be silly.'' It was a July Fourth tradition with the McKeons. He kissed the top of her head. "Got your master's yet?''

"Close.'' She pulled out of his arms as their parents

crowded forward. "I've got the rough draft done on my thesis, but it still needs a lot of work."

"Oh, work, work!" his mother complained, standing on tiptoe to enfold him. She was short and plump, and a tireless bully about her family's welfare. "This is supposed to be a holiday. No one should even be thinking about work."

"That's easy to say when you're retired." Darrick put his hands on her shoulders and drew her back as their father moved in to take her place in Duncan's embrace.

"A mother is never retired." She gave Darrick a dry glance over her shoulder. "And with you four, the work just goes on and on."

"How are you, son?" Duncan's father hugged him fiercely, then stepped back to look him over. "You're a little later than we expected. Everything all right?"

Duncan nodded, smiling into the warmly familiar faces around him. For a moment he forgot all the other people in the group that he didn't know, and just enjoyed the sense of comfort that settled over him whenever the McKeons gathered.

He knew that for many people, family get-togethers could be a chore rather than the cheerful reunions they were intended to be. But his family was special. With their strong personalities, they often disagreed, told each other off, fought it out, then found a way to compromise, or, if that was impossible, to accept. They shared a love forged of equal parts laughter and grief. Nothing could shake it.

"Yeah," he replied as they gathered unconsciously into a tight circle. "Everything's great. In fact, I'm late because Steven Spielberg picked me up at JFK."

There was a moment of stunned silence.

"You're kidding," Darrick finally said.

"No, I'm not. He's casting for a new film on Arthur and Guinevere."

"Aren't you a little old to be Mordred?" Dori asked abruptly, then apparently realizing how that sounded, smiled in apology. "You know what I mean."

He aimed a playful fist at her nose. "Actually, he wants me for Arthur."

"All *right!*" Dillon punched his arm. "Success at last! You finally get to be the hero."

"What do you mean, 'at last'?" Harper came into their midst to offer her hand. She was small and blond and lit up the space around her. "He's been a major heartthrob for years. Remember me? Harper Harriman?"

Duncan took her small hand in his. "I do. But I thought…" He looked from her to Dillon, not certain how to say that from what he'd last heard, their relationship was kaput.

Dillon came up from behind to wrap his arms around her. "We made up. In fact, we're getting married. You got home just in time."

Duncan looked at Darrick with a shake of his head. "Have you tried to talk her out of it?"

Darrick shrugged. "She wouldn't listen. She's found something about him to love. I don't understand it, but there's no accounting for—" He was stopped mid-sentence by Dillon's backhand to his solar plexus.

Duncan leaned down to kiss Harper's cheek. "Well, if you don't have better sense, then you're going to fit right in around here. Welcome to the family."

"Thank you." She made a beckoning gesture toward a group of ladies standing behind Dillon. The group parted to allow them in. "Duncan, I'd like you to meet my aunts Gracie and Edith,'' she said, pointing to two very pretty ladies he guessed to be in their early fifties. "They're going to be on Broadway in Portrait in a Penthouse."

He knew of the project: Bernie Kohler was one of the most respected directors in theater. Duncan offered the women sincere congratulations.

"And this is Aggie," Harper went on, indicating a small, gray-haired, pixieish woman probably a little older than her sisters. "She's an agent, and arranged for their auditions. And that's Aunt Phyllis." She pointed to a woman on crutches. "Knee-replacement surgery," she said by way of explanation. "She used to do voice-overs for television. Now she mostly does community theater."

Phyllis pointed to her leg in its cast. "I'm waiting for someone to remake *Rear Window* with a female lead."

He laughed. "Now there's an idea."

"And this is Cleo." Harper waved a hand toward the tallest of the group. "She's writing a book about their youth as the Stratton Sisters. They entertained with Bob Hope a few times."

"So I've been out-starred," Duncan said ruefully. Then he focused on the dark-haired toddler Cleo held in her arms.

"Who's this little guy?"

Dillon opened his mouth to reply just as the child leaned out of Cleo's arms toward him with a very possessive, "Da-da!"

Duncan watched his brother take the little boy, pride unmistakable in Dillon's eyes.

"Yes," Dillon said with a grin. "Darian. Your nephew."

Duncan absorbed the shock as he touched a small hand clutching Dillon's shirt sleeve. "No kidding?"

"No kidding."

"Well. As usual, you've performed with your customary brilliance. He's beautiful."

Gracie took an eager step forward as Darian wriggled to get down and went to play with a dog Duncan also didn't recognize.

"Speaking of performing with brilliance," she said, "when do you start filming with Spielberg?"

Hands in his pockets, Duncan lifted his shoulders to express indecision. "I don't think I will be."

"Why not?" Edith, too, came forward a step. "It's…Steven Spielberg!" There was awe in her voice.

He nodded. "I'm just not sure it's wise to put a villain in a hero's role. It'd be sad if miscasting botched the film for him."

Gracie eyed him curiously. "But you *act* the villain," she said reasonably. "And if you do it so well that one of the most successful directors of our time is after you, you can certainly act the hero. Can't you?"

He smiled, hoping to discourage her enthusiasm. He didn't want to talk about that now. It was impossible to explain to anyone his personal vision of himself. "Thank you. I appreciate that you think so."

"But—" Gracie began to offer more argument.

Edith elbowed her. "It's not your business," she said.

Gracie took exception to that. "Pardon me, but I've seen every film he's ever made and I'm telling you that the success of his villains is the fact that everyone watching knows there's a hero inside if he'll only let

him out." She sighed and patted his arm. "Sounds to
me like this is your chance. But I hate people who tell
me what to do, so I'll say no more."

Her sisters made sounds of scorn.

"She'll bring it up every chance she gets," Edith
warned under her breath.

Gracie subsided with wounded dignity.

Duncan turned back to his family and found himself
face to face with two more strangers: a beautiful brunette and a fair-haired boy of five or six with a buzz
cut and glasses.

The brunette's arms came around him in a warm
hug. "I'm Skye," she said, then drawing back, indicated the boy. "And this is David."

Duncan leaned down to shake the boy's hand. "David who?"

"McKeon," the boy replied. "Just like you. You're
my uncle." He pointed to Skye. "She's my mom and
he—" he turned around, apparently in search of someone, then pointed to Darrick "—he's my dad. And I
think the babies are sapposta be yours."

As Duncan tried to assimilate the meaning of the
boy's own family connections, he almost missed the
last bit of information. But the general gasp that followed it, and Skye's sudden covering of the boy's
mouth with her hand, made Duncan's mind repeat
what he'd heard.

And I think the babies are supposed to be yours.

What did that mean? What babies? He hadn't a clue.
But first things first.

"Okay, wait a minute," Duncan said as Darrick
came closer. Everyone else seemed to back away.
"One thing at a time." He focused on the brunette.
"What's *your* last name?"

"McKeon," she replied, her voice a little high, the easy warmth of a moment ago replaced by a curious nervousness that seemed to have overtaken everyone. Then she repeated the boy's words with a small smile. "Just like yours."

"Yes. So if you're this boy's mother, and Darrick is this boy's father, you and Darrick—"

She was nodding before he'd finished. "Are married. Yes. No one knew when you and Dillon were coming home so we just…did it. And we're adopting David."

"I see." He glanced at Darrick, who was eyeing him without the prevailing nervousness, but with a certain steadiness that Duncan knew from experience usually preceded some sort of revelation. And Duncan had the uneasy feeling he wasn't going to like what he was about to hear.

But how could he possibly be unhappy over the news that Darrick had gotten married and acquired a child? Unless they thought that because they'd always been so close and both his brothers were suddenly family men, that Duncan would feel disappointed at not being informed beforehand.

Duncan gently removed Skye's hand from David's mouth. "This boy's going to need to breathe." He winked at the boy, looking down into his bright blue eyes. David's coloring was all wrong for a McKeon, but the lively spirit seemed right.

"That's wonderful news." Duncan hugged Skye, then the boy. "But what was that about babies?"

"Darling!" his mother interrupted, pushing forward a nice-looking older couple about his parents' ages. "These are your neighbors here—Cliff and Bertie Fisher."

Each of the Fishers was holding a small baby.

"Hello." Duncan looked from the man to the woman in perplexity. They, too, were wearing the nervous expressions everyone else had suddenly adopted, but they smiled politely.

"How nice to have you home," the woman said. "We've been hearing so much about the famous Duncan."

The man, cradling a baby in one arm, used the other hand to point up the hill and to the right. "We live in the yellow house. Feel free to call us or come over at any time. We've gotten quite experienced...I mean, the babies have grown used to...ah..." He stammered and glanced at his wife, who gave him a quick shake of her head.

Cliff finally sighed and handed him the baby he held. "This is Michelle," he said.

Bertie put her baby in his other arm, and he had little choice but to accommodate the second small bundle. "And this is Gabrielle," she said, seemingly anxious to get away. "Excuse us. We...ah..." Bertie pointed to the group that was now making a mass exodus toward the house, and followed them without explanation. "Bye," she said simply.

Only Darrick and Dillon remained.

"Michelle and Gabrielle who?" Duncan called after Bertie.

"McKeon," Dillon replied.

Darrick patted him consolingly on the shoulder. "Just like *you*," he said.

Duncan froze, staring down at the tiny bundles. They appeared to be sleeping, their tiny, feathery lashes fanned on soft pink cheeks. Then he noticed the thick, almost comically spiked black hair on each little head and was reminded of someone else with thick dark hair—only there'd been nothing comical about it. It had been silky and luxurious as it skimmed down his body.

His heart boomed against his side with his sudden awakening to truth.

Oh, my God! he thought.

Chapter Two

The human heart is a well-catalogued repository of every emotion experienced in a lifetime. Actors and artists knew that and used it.

Duncan wondered how he would catalogue for later use what he felt now. Confusion? Consternation? Terror?

No. He had to be honest with himself. He felt some of those things, of course, but what he experienced foremost was relief. He didn't even need time to absorb the shock.

It was proof—finally!—that that night in Mexico had happened after all.

"Here, let me take one of the girls," Darrick offered, slipping his hand in between Duncan's arm and Michelle's head.

"No." Duncan said sharply.

Darrick looked up at him in surprise.

"Thanks, but no," Duncan repeated more quietly. The babies were a tie to her. He looked around him eagerly. "Where is she? Where's their mother?"

"Ah…that's kind of a long story."

"You mean she isn't here?"

"Right."

He experienced instant and acute disappointment. "Then where is she?"

Darrick sighed. "Dunk, it's all kind of mysterious. We'll tell you what we know, but...*can* they be yours?"

"How old are they?" he asked in response.

"Two months," Dillon replied, coming up on his other side to study them. His expression was curiously grim. "They were born a month premature, but they're perfect."

Duncan calculated. Yes. It had to be. September. The wrap party. A moonlit tropical night. A gnawing pain in his shoulder from a fall from a high-strung stallion, an injection of some fast-acting pain medication.

All the cast and crew had been high with the excitement of having the tedious, exhausting, demanding process of making a movie finally completed. His agent had flown in to discuss the next project with him, and had hosted a party at a local cantina. She sat at Duncan's table, along with his co-star and a camerawoman who played poker better than any man he'd ever met.

He remembered everything clearly until the second glass of champagne, then it all began to blur. He remembered the feeling of good cheer, of satisfaction, of accomplishment. Then the conversation turned to families...and that had brought thoughts of Donovan.

That was when he'd remembered it all—really remembered—for the first time in years. The painful memory of Donovan, his little brother, stricken by leukemia, fading away to nothing until he was just a skeletal little creature in a small, satin-lined box, had melded with the pain in Duncan's shoulder, and had overpowered him.

And he'd poured out the pain to someone—a woman. Then there'd been a soothing hand on his brow and a surprisingly strong arm around him, leading him as they walked uphill—or had it been upstairs?

Then he'd held her, undressed her. He had no clear memory of doing so, but a kind of tactile recollection of satiny skin against his fingertips, of lips on his pectoral muscles, of long, silky hair following those lips on a quest down the middle of his body.

It had been a tenderly intimate experience and a cosmically erotic one. He'd felt humbled and changed by it.

Until he'd awakened alone the following morning with a killer headache—unable to put a face to the woman with whom he'd made love. He'd stared at his own face in the pocked bathroom mirror off the spartan but tidy little room above the taverna, and had wondered if *she* was somewhere in Puerta Flora right now wondering what *he* looked like.

He'd put a hand to his aching head and groaned, considering that in view of his physical state the night before, it was probably best if she'd forgotten him. He couldn't have put in much of a performance.

Then someone had banged on his door and told him the bus was leaving for the airport in five minutes.

On the bus, none of the women who'd been at his table the night before behaved with any reticence. Jeanine Curry, the camerawoman, had demanded the ten bucks he owed her from the last poker game; Yvette Delacroix, his co-star, talked animatedly about the publicity stills they'd be shooting in two weeks' time; and Phoebe Price, his agent, had discussed the next project with her customary detachment and professional attention to detail.

By the time he'd gotten to his parents' anniversary party in San Diego, where his siblings had gathered, he'd almost convinced himself that he'd dreamed the entire scenario. That the intensity of the emotional memory had simply been a reaction to months of celibacy and his vulnerability after talking about Donovan's death.

Then the dreams had begun. Velvet, opulent dreams of touch and tenderness, of soft whispers and warm kisses, of satin threads of hair dragging across his face, over his shoulders, his ribs, his belly.

He would awaken in the darkness and reach for her—only to find himself in his lonely king-size bed in his mansion in Malibu, or in his single bed in some remote filming location.

He'd concluded that something that was so rooted in his subconscious that he dreamed of it over and over *had* to have some basis in fact.

And now he had proof. Double proof. God.

"Yes," he said finally, in answer to Darrick's question. "They could be mine."

Darrick and Dillon stared at him a long moment, then exchanged looks of relief.

"You're sure?" Dillon asked.

Duncan shrugged a shoulder. "Well…I'm not sure of anything, except that I did make love with a woman at the time they would have been conceived."

"An actress?" Dillon again.

"I don't know."

"You don't know if she was an actress, or you don't know if the actress was the one?"

He sighed and admitted reluctantly, "I don't know who it was I made love with."

That statement earned the complete silence it deserved.

"Okay," Darrick said finally, pulling up a lawn chair. "Sit down, and we'll tell you what we know."

Duncan sat, noting absently that late afternoon had evolved into evening, though the breeze off the ocean remained warm.

His brothers hovered protectively around the babies, guiding Duncan into a chair.

"You know," he said, "I don't recall you two being such fussy hens."

"We've become fathers," Dillon explained, tucking Gabrielle's blanket in around her. "It changes you."

Duncan watched his brothers pull up chairs on either side of him.

"Well..." Dillon angled one leg over the other and cast a concerned look at Darrick. "You should start," he said to him, "because you were the first to see them."

"See who?" Duncan asked.

"Michelle and Gabrielle," Darrick replied.

As Duncan prepared to ask another question, Darrick forestalled him with a raised hand. "Let me tell you what I know, then you can ask all the questions you want. You sure you don't want one of us to hold one of the babies?"

"I'm sure. Just start talking."

"All right." Darrick drew a breath, stretched his feet out before him, crossed his ankles and lifted his face to the breeze. Then he closed his eyes, as though organizing his thoughts. It always amazed Duncan that thoughts could be organized. His were always all over the place. "Early in May, I spent a long weekend at a hospital conference and came home to discover that while I was gone a young woman was admitted to Valley Memorial and gave birth to twins."

Duncan felt a glimmer of hope. "So we *know* who she is."

Darrick replied patiently, "No, we don't. The name she gave us wasn't her real name. She abandoned the twins on the second day."

Duncan opened his mouth to demand to know how that could have happened, but Darrick stopped him again. "I know. That doesn't seem possible. But it happened. I was gone, remember? Anyway, everybody at the hospital thought the babies were mine because the name on the birth certificate was D. K. McKeon. And there was a while there when I thought they were mine, too. I couldn't reach you or Dillon, so I brought the twins home with me."

"You thought they were Maddie Hale's?"

"No," Darrick corrected. "We'd broken up long before that. I thought they were Skye's. Remember the light plane crash that made me late for Mom and Dad's anniversary party?" When Duncan nodded, he went on, "Skye was the pilot. And we...well."

Duncan studied him in disbelief. "The two of you had just survived a plane crash in the mountains and you made love?"

"It was cold," Darrick explained thinly. "We were trying to keep each other warm."

"By taking all their clothes off," Dillon contributed helpfully.

Darrick silenced him with a look, then carried on with his explanation. "Right after I finally figured out that the twins weren't mine, Dillon came home. His medical team had been in Nicaragua, helping victims of an earthquake. He thought the twins might be his.''

"Harper's?" Duncan asked.

"That was a possibility." Dillon nodded. "But now we know they're not. So…" He spread both arms in a "therefore" gesture. "They *must* be yours."

Duncan looked down at the babies in his arms—both once more fast asleep—and felt certain that they were.

"I think so," he agreed quietly.

"How is it that you don't know who their mother is?" Darrick asked bluntly.

Duncan explained about the wrap party and the pain medication. He frowned as he tried to think back. He couldn't believe memories of her touch could be so clear, while he had no memory at all of her face.

"I remember…that we made love," he said, his gaze unfocused as he concentrated. He could feel her fingertips even now. "I remember that she was kind and empathetic and sweet. I just don't remember her face."

There was another moment's silence, then Dillon groaned. "I don't believe it. We finally figure out that Duncan is Michelle and Gabrielle's father, but he doesn't know who their mother is. So the poor babies still have no real parents."

"Yes, they do," Duncan said. "They have me. They have a father."

The words sounded heroic, and he was enough of a thespian to appreciate a well-spoken line. But even *he* was a little surprised at how deeply he meant them.

He had no idea how he was going to care for two babies with the kind of life he led, but he wasn't going to worry about that right now. They were a link to *her,* a way to find her. Somehow.

"Did someone at the hospital have a description of the mother?" Duncan asked Darrick.

"It's pretty sketchy," Darrick answered. "Her chart says she was 5'4", age 26, and weighing 157 when she was admitted. 'Course, a lot of that was babies. The nurses remember her as small-boned and quiet, and that she had dark hair."

Duncan tried to relate that description to one of the women who'd sat at his table that night. It *had* to be one of them, he thought. He recalled that everyone else at the party had gone out skinny-dipping, but he and the women at his table had been deeply involved in a discussion about his next project.

"Not much to go on," he said. Particularly since it fit every woman with whom he'd partied that night. Yvette was blond, but changed her hair color from film to film. Phoebe was plumper than the description, and ten years older than he, but could easily pass for younger. Jeanine was hardly quiet, but he supposed labor could dull any woman's vivacity.

"What are you going to do?" Dillon asked.

Duncan didn't even have to think about it. "I'm going to find her."

"How?" Darrick wanted to know.

"I guess…I'll just have to locate the women at my table that night until I find the one who had the twins."

"And then what?" his brothers asked simultaneously.

He frowned from one to the other. "Then…I'll hire William Goldman to write me a happy ending— How do *I* know?"

Dillon raised both hands placatingly. "You're forgetting that you can't run around the country—or maybe the globe, considering your circle of friends—with a pair of two-month-old babies."

Valid point. "What did you do," he asked Darrick, "when you first brought them home from the hospital? I presume Skye wasn't around yet?"

"Right. But fortunately for me, Dori had just come home from Oxford and stopped by to see me on her way home to San Diego. So I hired her to stay with me while she worked on her thesis."

"She's a good nanny," Dillon said. "She stayed on to work for me, but she's not what you'd call dependable. I mean, she's gone at the drop of a hat to all these various appointments related to her thesis. So you're going to need an alternative plan."

"Dunk, do you know enough about babies to do this?" Darrick's tone expressed deep concern. "Dillon, at least, was a doctor and used to caring for babies in his work."

"But you weren't," Duncan pointed out, annoyed. "A hospital administrator isn't exactly a day-care provider. Don't worry about it. I *played* a father once."

Dillon rolled his eyes. "In *Chosen Children?* You were an alcoholic who ended up with three kids after his ex-wife died. They were taken away from you."

Duncan shook his head at him. "Only in the script. On the set, I got very close to those kids."

"And sent them home at the end of the day to their parents. Two-month-old babies are a twenty-four-hour-a-day job."

"Twenty-five," Darrick corrected.

"Guys, listen." Duncan sat up in his chair, trying to use the severe look that used to intimidate his brothers when they'd all been children. It was a little harder to carry off with two babies wrapped in pink blankets in his arms—but he was a good actor. "I know you've always thought I was softer than you because there are more luxuries in my life. And you think my work is considerably easier than yours, and far more superficial. In some ways it is. I don't go from one world crisis to another like you, Dill. And I'm not responsible for the dispersion of millions of dollars and the organization of a network of people and equipment that save lives like Darrick..."

Duncan took a deep breath, a little surprised to hear all this coming out of him. He never felt the need to justify what he did because when he really struck the art of it, it touched lives and sometimes had the power to change them. But there was obviously some insecurity at work here.

He tried to put the thought out of his mind and plunged on. "I work long hours, in often rotten conditions, taking on someone else's angst and grief, and to do that I have to understand life and people to a degree you probably don't have to very often. I don't put it on the same level as what you two do for a living. But when it comes to understanding what's inside people's souls rather than inside their bodies, I *might* be better at it than you are. I *can* be a father."

Darrick stared at him, apparently also surprised by the outburst. Then he said reasonably, "And that would be very useful if you were dealing with a couple of moody and confused adolescent girls—but you're not. You're dealing with little babies who need you to understand their physical needs as well as their emotional ones."

"I'm sure I'll learn." He looked from one brother

to the other. "Have a little faith in me, will you? Who pulled the two of you out of scrapes our entire childhood? And who found you berries to eat when we got lost on that hiking trail in Colorado?"

Dillon put a hand over his eyes. "Promise me you won't feed the twins berries."

Both arms occupied, Duncan reached out a foot and kicked him in the shin. "We're going to be fine. And you'll be around for another day to help me out."

"Actually," Dillon corrected, rubbing his shin, "we'll all be around an extra two days. Harper and I are getting married on Monday while we're all together."

Duncan felt a strange ripple in the predictable pattern of his life. Darrick was married and adopting a son. Dillon was about to be married and had a toddler. And he, Duncan, had twin babies. God. The change all this would create in their connected lives was bound to be enormous.

The three of them had spent a lot of time apart since they'd all started going off to school, but when they did come together on holidays or during the summer, they were always each other's first priority.

That would be different now. They had wives. Children. Duncan experienced a strange sense of alienation—a feeling seldom known in this family.

Darrick leaned toward him. "So you're still going to stay here for the month of July? If you'd rather, you're welcome to come home with Skye and David and me. You can use our place as a base of operations while you try to find the women who were at your table that night."

"Thanks. But I'm sure I'll be fine. I'll talk to Dori about helping me out." Suddenly Duncan noticed that neither brother was looking at him. Two pairs of concerned dark eyes were focused on the babies with a pain in them he didn't understand for a moment. Then he remembered that first Darrick, then Dillon, had thought for a while that the twins were theirs. They'd loved these babies, and now, after Dillon's wedding on Monday, they had to leave.

"I'm sorry," he said gravely, "that my actions so upset your lives."

Both looked up at him in surprise.

Darrick shook his head and smiled slowly. "I wouldn't have missed it for anything."

"Me, neither." Dillon, who'd apparently only just found out the babies weren't his, was obviously dealing with fresher pain. His voice broke, and Darrick leaned across their little circle to touch his arm.

"I promise you I won't feed them berries or otherwise endanger them." He kicked Dillon again, but gently this time. "I'll take good care of them."

"Boys!" Peg McKeon called from the back porch. "I've got coffee on, and we're forming teams for Trivial Pursuit."

Duncan groaned. "I hate that game," he said under his breath.

"It's the silver-screen edition!" Peg added.

"Well, that changes everything." Duncan stood and this time tolerated the attentions of his brothers as each moved to protect one of the babies and to support him while he got to his feet.

HE WASN'T SURPRISED to discover that he wasn't quite as adept at fatherhood as he'd anticipated—at least, the "what, please God, are they screaming about" part of it.

He'd excused himself from the living room when one of the babies awoke and her crying woke the other. He now stood in the middle of the kitchen, wondering what to do.

He placed the twins in a single carrier because Darrick told him they liked being together, then went to the refrigerator where Dillon told him the bottles were kept.

"Just run the bottles under hot-water to warm them up a little!" Skye had shouted after him.

While Duncan worked, he reflected that his line about what he'd learned as an actor preparing him to relate to children had been all bluff. As had been much of his big-brothering when he and Darrick and Dillon were boys.

As a young child, he'd been very good at being the oldest. He knew things his brothers didn't because he'd experienced them before—and that had given him confidence. Their adoration of him and the responsibility that brought with it gave him courage.

Then Donovan had gotten sick, and everything changed. Duncan had never been sick before. At least, not so sick that his ribs showed, and his skin color changed, and his hair fell out. And there'd been absolutely nothing Duncan could do.

He'd been ten years old. And by then, in his eight-year career as a big brother, he'd saved a life or two, he'd averted injuries or tended them if they'd been unavoidable. He'd calmed fears, stood in the way of bullies, cheered, derided, encouraged, and condemned.

But now he was powerless. He'd nagged his parents about going to a different doctor, a different hospital—and finally they'd sat him and Darrick and Dillon down and explained tearfully that Donovan was dying and that there was nothing anyone could do to stop it.

They'd all sobbed together, and Dillon had asked if they could all die so they could go with Donovan. Then their mother had become nearly hysterical and their father had had to take her from the room.

His brothers had wanted to know what Duncan was going to do about it.

The next day, after school, Duncan had taken them to see Donovan's doctor. They'd made it clear to the physician that they wanted their brother cured—and *quickly.*

He'd taken them into his office, closed the door, and explained kindly that everything that *could* be done *had* been done, but that no one could make Donovan better. Then he'd gathered them all around his chair and told them that sometimes when you loved someone very much, the best thing you could do for them was to travel with them as far as you were able, and then to let them go.

And that was what they'd done. They'd played quiet games with Donovan as long as he was up to playing. Then, when he grew too weak, they simply sat beside his bed and talked about baseball and astronauts.

Then he went back into the hospital.

And then he was gone.

Duncan rallied his remaining brothers, and they formed a new alliance curiously enriched by mutual suffering and loss.

Then Dori was born. At first the boys had been indignant about the presence of a girl in their midst, but she'd been beautiful and interesting and spirited enough to negate their customary no-girls rule. As she grew, they'd gathered protectively around her so that

the four of them became a unit, ignoring her claim
that their guardianship denied her the equality she
craved and relegated her to a lower status.

"So you're the one who's blessed your father and
me with granddaughters?" His mother appeared in the
kitchen, forcing aside his thoughts. She took the bottle
he'd warmed under the faucet and went to one of the
babies. He couldn't tell yet which was which. She
picked the infant up, settled into a kitchen chair, and
gave her the bottle. The screeching sound that filled
the kitchen was cut instantly in half.

"Michelle's the one who always screams first and
loudest," Peg said to Duncan as she adjusted herself
and the baby comfortably. "So we tend to pick her up
first because it's easier to get her quiet. I suppose that
isn't good for Gabrielle, and we should stop doing it.
But Gabrielle's generally such a laid-back baby, she
might not even notice."

"I still can't tell who's who," Duncan admitted,
turning off the hot-water faucet and taking the other
warmed bottle to the table. He put it down, picked up
the second baby, and put the nipple to her wide-open
mouth. The moment she perceived what it was, her
little lips tightened around it and a blessed silence
reigned while she sucked greedily.

"So I have *Gabrielle*." He hooked a chair with his
foot and drew it back so that he could sit opposite his
mother.

"Yes." She put an index finger under a tiny hand
on the baby she held, and showed him the red mark
on a little fingernail. "One of the nurses marked it
with Skin Scribe in the hospital, so Darrick could tell
who was who when he brought them home. He and
Dillon decided to keep doing it until something hap-

pens in their features to allow us to distinguish them physically. When they're awake, you can usually tell which is which, but when they're asleep, it's impossible.''

Gabrielle's brown eyes focused on Duncan as she ate, and her little fingers worked. He put his index finger to her hand and watched, fascinated, as her fingers closed over it and gripped.

Something inside him melted.

Then he looked up to answer his mother's question. ''Yes, I am responsible for your granddaughters.'' He explained briefly about the party in the cantina and the pain medication that made it impossible for him to remember who the mother was. Then he felt compelled to add, ''It wasn't random or thoughtless sex. We were all talking about families and I was feeling no pain from the medication and a glass of champagne. Then I told her about Donovan...'' He expelled a breath. ''And the pain of that made it through. She was comforting and gentle and...I just don't remember any more.''

His mother studied him with that look that could still read the state of his health and his every thought. He braced himself for a lecture on the grave status of modern morals, but she apparently chose to sidestep that angle of the problem altogether.

''If you're going to stay here for the month of July,'' she said practically, ''you're going to need someone to help you with the babies.''

He nodded. ''Darrick and Dillon have already briefed me. I thought I'd ask Dori if she'll stay.''

As though on cue, Dori burst out of the downstairs bedroom where she'd sequestered herself with a phone call, and sat in the chair facing Duncan. Her eyes were bright, her cheeks pink. "You'll never guess what just happened!" she declared.

"Then maybe you'd better tell us," his mother said serenely, then added with a wry smile, "remembering, of course, that I suffer from high blood pressure *and* paranoia."

Dori leaned toward her on one elbow. "You know that woman I've been e-mailing in Halifax? The one who wrote that Jane Austen biography I admired so much?"

"No."

"Well, anyway, she's great. She's helped me with a lot of details, and she's invited me to come and stay for the next two weeks to talk about my thesis. Isn't that wonderful?"

Peg looked at Duncan.

Duncan made himself smile. "It's wonderful."

Dori frowned suddenly, apparently realizing the implications of her sudden trip. "Uh, oh. You're going to be alone with two babies until I get back."

"That's not your problem," he said magnanimously. "Go and do your thing. I'll find someone to help."

"Well, nannies are quite the thing now," Peg said. "There has to be a local service that could help you, Duncan."

He nodded. "I'll check into it in the morning."

Dori snapped her fingers. "I know!" She closed her eyes in concentration. "Oh, this would be so perfect. Ariel Bonneau!"

"Who?" he asked.

"Ariel Bonneau," she repeated. "We were at UCLA together for the first couple of years, then she left to enter the convent."

Duncan panicked at the thought of a nun in his house.

"Dori, this isn't *The Sound of Music*, okay. I don't want to derail some poor nun."

She made a face at him. "She's not a nun anymore. She wrote me when she came out two months ago. She said she hasn't found a permanent job yet. She'd be perfect! Oh, Dunk—" she leaned over the baby to touch his shoulder "—you'd love her. And so would the twins! She's gentle and sweet and very..." She made an indeterminate gesture with her right hand.

"Strange?" he guessed.

"No."

"Ugly?"

"No!"

"Repressed?"

"Duncan, she's none of those things," she said, the hand that had touched his shoulder now swatting it. "She's great. She just has to get her life together again. You know. Relearn the outside world."

"You think confining her with two tiny babies would do that?"

Dori looked around her at the kitchen, which Duncan had to admit looked considerably better than it had when he and his brothers had bought the house months ago. The agreement had been that the Realtor would arrange to have the outside of the house painted; Darrick would make small repairs and paint the inside during his month's vacation; Dillon, who was artistic as well as brilliant, would buy furniture out of the fund they'd established; and Duncan would landscape and buy lawn furniture.

"This is such a great place," Dori said with sudden seriousness. "I think it'd be a wonderful, peaceful spot

for her to…collect herself." She grinned just as suddenly. "And you can be okay company when you
try."

"That sounds like a plan," Peg said. "Duncan,
you'll have to have someone around if you're going
to go looking for your women."

The censure he'd expected when he'd first told her
about the party in the cantina, now took shape in the
smallest intonation in her voice. "They're not *my*
women, Mom. They're friends who were all there that
night."

"I understand."

She didn't, but then neither did he entirely. So he
just let it drop.

"How do I get in touch with this Ariel?" he asked
Dori.

"Want me to call her," she asked, "so you can talk
to her yourself and see what you think?"

"Ah…sure."

Dori was gone like a shot.

Michelle had finished eating, and Peg put her to her
shoulder and patted her back. Duncan tried to copy his
mother's movements, but Gabrielle screeched at him.

"Gabrielle has a bigger appetite," Peg explained.

Duncan put the nipple back into the baby's mouth
and she settled down again. "A munch mouth, huh?"
he said to Gabrielle, and was rewarded with a smile
around the nipple and a kick in the gut. He felt weak.

"You think you're going to be able to cope?" Peg
asked.

He gave his mother a reprimanding look. "Of
course." The bluff he'd always used on his brothers
extended to his parents as well. He just wasn't as sure

with them that he'd always pulled it off. "You know that I'm determined and capable."

She smiled at him. "I do. I also know that you feel responsible for everyone's well-being and safety, and for the success of all their projects. With your own children, that attitude can be exhausting and heart-rending. You'll have to pace yourself."

"I'll be fine, Mom."

She nodded and smiled again. "I know you will be, Duncan."

Dori handed him the telephone and took Gabrielle from him. Then she shooed him toward the privacy of his parents' downstairs bedroom.

He closed the door behind him. "Hello?" he said, wandering toward the window. It was now dark beyond the windows and he could see one lonely light way out on the ocean. He related to it.

"Yes, hello," a warm feminine voice replied. It was quiet but animated. "Is this…Duncan?"

"Yes. And you're Ariel."

"Yes."

So far so good. The fact that she was a friend of Dori's precluded the formality that might otherwise insulate the first employer-nanny conversation. But what did one ask a nanny, anyway?

"Do you have experience with babies?" he asked.

"Ah…actually, I don't," she replied, reluctance in her voice. "But I like people in general, and children in particular. And I'm generally calm and patient." She laughed softly. "And modest."

He laughed, too. "Are you able to relocate? I'm not certain how long the job will last. And I might have to leave you alone with the babies for several days at a time while I travel."

"That'd be no problem," she said. "I live alone; there's no one to answer to."

"*Where* do you live?" he asked.

"Southern California," she replied.

"Dancer's Beach is considerably quieter than any-where in southern California," he felt compelled to warn her. "Do you think you can deal with that?"

She laughed again. "I've been living in a convent, Duncan," she said.

He also had to laugh again. "Point well taken." Then he said candidly, "You know, I have to admit that I'm a little...concerned about that. I don't have a very spiritual turn of mind."

"I promise not to bless you, or anything."

"Good."

"And if we're being honest, I'm a little intimidated by who you are, too. I mean..." She paused, then said as though she were underlining it, "*Duncan McKeon. The definitive Iago, the best Sheriff of Nottingham, the greatest Dr. Moriarty...*"

Of course. He hadn't thought of that. "You're wor-ried about aligning yourself with a portrayer of evil."

There was a moment's pause, then, sounding sur-prised that he'd made such a suggestion, she replied, "Not at all. I just mean...I mean, you're a *movie star*. And not just a pretty face or great pecs, but someone with talent who deserves all that acclaim."

Even while he wondered if the "not just a pretty face" remark meant that he had other qualities as well, or that he simply *didn't* have a pretty face, he puzzled more over a nun talking about pecs. Then he remem-bered that she was an ex-nun.

And she *had* said that he was talented.

He mentioned a salary. She said that she thought it was more than generous.

She sounded serene—and agreeable. It occurred to him that that might be a change he'd be ready for when his inquisitive and challenging family left. So he asked, "When could you be here?"

"When would you need me?"

"Can you be here day after tomorrow? Maybe sometime in the afternoon? There's a wedding going on here in the morning."

"Yours?"

"My brother's. I'll make reservations for you. Dori will call you back and let you know your flight number and time. There's a small commuter service from Portland to Dancer's Beach. I'll pick you up at the airport here. Is there anything you'd like to ask? Anything else you need?"

"No, I think we've covered everything. I'll see you Monday afternoon."

"Yes. Monday afternoon."

Duncan turned off the phone and stared into the darkness with its one pinpoint of light.

He'd always felt that way about life—as though somewhere out there was the place he belonged, or the person he was supposed to be.

It wasn't that he didn't love his family and feel completely a part of their tight circle. Nor was it that he wasn't pleased with and grateful for his career, which had taken him higher and farther than he'd ever hoped to go when he showed up in Los Angeles with four-hundred dollars and an appointment to audition for a soap opera.

He wasn't really sure what nagged at him, but some vague discontent stood in his way at the end of every day. Now that he had a quiet moment to think about it, he realized that this had begun right after the filming in Mexico.

He could only conclude that it was *her*—his mystery woman—whoever she was. She'd soothed away his pain that night, then disappeared.

But apparently he'd given her something, too.

If he stopped to think about it, the awesome responsibility of two fragile little lives was enough to make him want to run in the other direction, lose himself in another film.

But he thought about her instead, and wondered why she hadn't simply come to him and told him that she was pregnant. Or why she hadn't stayed with the babies and waited for him to come back from Africa. Why had she run away?

He remembered the tenderness of her touch, the gentle whispers in his ear, the generosity of her response to him. He couldn't reconcile those memories with thoughts of a woman who would abandon her babies to a man who didn't even know her name.

Then he smiled in the dark. No, he thought. She hadn't abandoned them. She was biding her time for some reason he didn't understand. She would come back.

Unless he found her first.

Chapter Three

Gabrielle played with her feet in the middle of Duncan's bed, her eyes and mouth round as she concentrated with complete fascination on her toes.

Beside her, Michelle flailed arms and legs with an enthusiasm that had already taught Duncan to keep his chin out of her way. While her little limbs moved, she gurgled and squealed—a lively, kinetic little bundle of sparkle and glow.

Duncan was half dressed in suit pants and a T-shirt, distracted from finishing the process by his daughters. *His daughters.* He felt a weird trembling in the pit of his stomach at the knowledge that these babies were his. They were so beautiful, so perfect, literally humming with intelligence and spirit.

Of course, they had few tools with which to express it yet, but their dark eyes watched him—maybe even *knew* him.

He stood to pull on his long-sleeved white shirt, leaning over them so that they could continue to watch him.

Thinking they knew him was strictly self-indulgence on his part, he realized. If they seemed to respond to him already, it had to be simply because he looked so much like his brothers, who'd already put in their stints as dads. The babies were probably mistaking him for one of them.

But whatever the reason, he loved the fact that after just a day and a half they grew animated when they saw him.

He'd held them all day yesterday while the family lazed around the house and in the backyard. Dori taught him to diaper; Skye taught him her tricks for quieting them when they fussed; Harper showed him their favorite rattles, and how they were learning to react with broad smiles to a new mobile over their crib.

His brothers eagerly relieved him of the babies so that he could eat, take a walk, relax. And his parents simply bullied them away from him every once in a while, claiming that since they'd be leaving for home right after the wedding, they wanted to get in as much spoiling as possible.

Duncan wondered if any two babies on the face of the earth had ever been so loved and so fussed over.

"Duncan!" His father hurried into the room, looking curiously alien in a dark suit and tie. A frown registered his disapproval of Duncan's dawdling. "Son," he said, spotting the tie on the arm of a chair and snatching it up, "I'm the first one to understand your fascination with your babies, but the minister will be here in five minutes, and you don't want your mother upset because you're the only one who isn't ready, do you?"

Duncan quickly buttoned his shirt and tucked the tail into his pants. "No, I don't," he agreed quickly, then thanked his father for the tie.

Duncan went to the mirror over the dresser to knot

it. His father's head was visible just beyond his own reflection.

"I'm glad you're pleased about the babies," Charlie said.

"It's hard to take exception to babies," Duncan replied, raising his shirt collar and adjusting the ends of the tie.

"They're probably going to play hell with your career. At least, until you find their mother."

"Not a problem."

"But I thought Spielberg wanted you to play King Arthur."

Duncan did all the ritualistic wrapping, slipping through, pulling down of the tie. "He does, but I'm not going to do it."

The knot was perfect, but Duncan gave it that final adjustment. Then, turning to reach for his jacket, he found himself confronted by his frowning father.

"Because of the twins?"

Duncan shook his head and walked around him to grab the jacket. "No. Because Arthur's the quintessential hero and I'm…the bad guy."

There was a knowing look in his father's eye that Duncan turned away from. Charlie caught his arm and pulled him back around.

Duncan tried again to divert him. "I thought we didn't want Mom coming in here and grumping at us."

"Right now you're more in danger of *me* grumping at you," Charlie said, his frown deepening. "I thought we resolved this when you were twelve and Dillon fell off the garage roof. You're the oldest, but you're not your siblings' guardian angel. You can't protect them from everything, and there was nothing you could have done about Donovan.'' Charlie held Duncan in place when he tried to pull loose. ''Duncan,'' he said reasonably, ''I know you know that.''

''Of course I do.'' Duncan remained still, putting all his energy into acting truthful. ''It has nothing to do with that.''

''Then, what does it have to do with?''

''Box office, Dad. The simple rules of what the audience will believe and what they won't believe. They don't accept Stallone in comedy, they don't like Eastwood in anything but heroic roles, and they believe in me as a villain because I'm a good one.''

''Why?''

''What do you mean, why? I just am. My first role was as a cad on a soap, and I discovered I had a gift for playing selfish and nasty. There's money in it, Dad. That defines everything in Hollywood.''

His father studied him a long moment and finally dropped his hands. Duncan knew that it wasn't because his father had given up on the argument, but because a woman's firm footsteps could be heard coming down the corridor.

''Money has never defined everything in you,'' Charlie insisted quietly as the footsteps drew nearer. ''You'd better think this through, son. Particularly if you're going to raise two little girls. You're going to have to know yourself better than you do.''

''Well, time has simply stood still so that the two of you can stand here and talk about what? Baseball?'' Duncan's mother burst into the room on a cloud of spicy perfume and righteous indignation. ''A backyard full of people and a very busy minister are waiting outside and here you two are…doing what?''

''Getting dressed,'' Charlie replied calmly. ''We'd

have come out naked just to be on time, but thought that might offend the minister. Stop shouting and take a baby.''

Charlie handed her Michelle and scooped up Gabrielle.

Peg held the baby, dressed in a ruffled sleeper, against her shoulder, and looked in concern from Charlie's set jaw to Duncan's carefully remote expression. "What *were* you talking about? Is something wrong?''

"Nothing's wrong." Duncan turned her toward the door. "Come on, Mom. You're holding us up."

With a growl of annoyance, she led the small parade down the stairs and outside.

His father winked at him as they followed. "Let's hope you learn to handle the twins as well as you handle your mother.''

Dillon and Harper were married under the brilliant green comb-like leaves of the backyard ash tree. The five aunts gave Harper away, and Duncan, Darrick, Dori and Skye bore witness as the uncharacteristically solemn couple promised to love and cherish each other.

Harper wore a gauzy white dress and a broad-brimmed white straw hat; Dillon, a dark suit. Duncan couldn't remember having seen him in one since they'd all gone to an uncle's wedding in their early teens.

As he watched them repeat their vows, he realized anew how much his brothers' lives had changed. Dillon had always been such a free spirit, a man driven to chase disasters and to comfort and heal the victims left behind.

Darrick had theorized that Dillon was trying to make up for having been unable to cure Donovan.

Duncan had agreed, seeing a similar reaction in Darrick. He spent his own life trying to out-organize disease and injury, keeping at optimum performance the small, suburban hospital he oversaw.

Duncan looked from one to the other now and saw that a new peace seemed to have settled over each of them. Darrick smiled across the small wedding party at Skye, who smiled back, her hair adorned with pink roses.

Dillon slipped a ring on Harper's finger, and they looked into each other's eyes with an expression of love so deep and intimate that Duncan had to look away.

He felt left behind. His brothers had dealt with their demons and learned to love.

What was wrong with *him*, anyway?

He didn't have time to think about it. The ceremony over, there was much cheering and crying and laughter and food.

He kept trying to reclaim the twins, but his parents had them and refused to relinquish them.

He shed his jacket and shot hoops with David into an apple basket Darrick had cut the bottom out of and nailed to the garage.

Then it was time to pick up Ariel Bonneau at the airport. The reception was winding down and food was being taken back inside. The bride and groom were changing clothes in preparation for a flight to New York with Harper's aunts, who were delivering Gracie and Edith to their new gig on Broadway.

Duncan borrowed Darrick's car and headed for Foxglove Field—nothing more than a vast open space across the highway from the ocean. Several light planes were lined up in an orderly row behind a long, angular building. A larger propeller plane, which he guessed represented most of the commuter airline's fleet, had parked just off the runway.

He was late. Not a good impression to make on a new employee. On an ex-nun.

He parked the car in a paved lot in front of the building.

Duncan hurried inside. About a dozen people milled around the small waiting area—some working, some waiting for a flight out or to be picked up.

He spotted Ariel instantly. She was tall and bony, short gray hair combed back in loose waves, her arms crossed, a long-suffering look of weariness on her face as she picked up a public telephone and prepared to dial.

"Miss Bonneau?" he called, striding toward her.

"Yes," a quiet voice replied from behind him.

Duncan turned in surprise.

A small, much younger woman stood before him in baggy jeans and a white cotton shirt. Of course. If she'd gone to school with Dori, she had to be younger. She was average in height and on the slender side. Her hair was short and her eyes very dark and unsettlingly wary.

He remembered Dori saying Ariel had been on the "outside" only two months, and that she was having a little difficulty adjusting. And Ariel had admitted to him on the phone that she was intimidated by what she'd called his "star status."

He'd always found it amusing that fans, and sometimes even his old friends, felt that his celebrity status somehow separated him from them. Sometimes the attention and the recognition were fun, sometimes they were annoying, but they never made any difference to what was important in his life—his family, his health, his spirit. Therefore, in most respects, he ignored it.

But he might have to turn on the charm to put her at ease. He smiled broadly, took her bag from her, and offered his hand. "Hi," he said, "I'm Duncan Mc-Keon."

She returned his smile a little nervously, then her wary eyes went from him to the circle of people around them. He hadn't noticed them until this moment, but it was as though some magnet had collected them from every corner of the terminal. He'd been recognized.

He smiled at them. They smiled back and pressed a little closer.

"Just...meeting a friend," he said, pulling Ariel into his arm as an eager man behind her reached over her shoulder and shoved an Oregon Coast tourist brochure at him.

"Would you sign this, Mr. McKeon? It'll restore my daughter's faith in me if you will. She's sixteen."

Duncan smiled apologetically at Ariel, put her bag down, and took the pen the man handed him. A woman held a paperback book under it so that Duncan could sign it without having to hold it.

"A *friend?*" the woman asked, studying Ariel with interest. "'Entertainment Tonight' said you weren't seeing anyone. That you love being a bachelor."

"I do," Duncan replied, now signing an envelope held out to him. The woman propped her book under it, too. "This is my nanny."

"Nanny?" the woman repeated on a high note. "You mean you have...children?"

"Two," he replied cheerfully. "Little girls, two months old."

"But…who is their mother?"

"My secret," he replied, leaning down to kiss the woman's cheek. She turned crimson, held a hand to it and giggled. "Thanks for your help." He looked up to smile at everyone. "Good to see you all. This young lady's probably very tired and I'd like to get her home now." He picked up Ariel's bag.

The little crowd followed him as far as the door, then fell into each other like dominoes when he turned and stopped them with a raised hand. "Goodbye," he said, and waved.

Everyone waved back.

Duncan saw Ariel into the front seat, then put her bag in the back. He climbed in behind the wheel, reversed out of the space and turned for home.

"You have good nerves." He pulled up at the stop sign and looked both ways before turning onto the highway. "Enthusiastic fans usually upset the people I'm with."

SHE STUDIED HIS handsome profile and had real difficulty dealing with her new reality. *Duncan McKeon.* She was in Dancer's Beach, Oregon, with Duncan McKeon.

After the years of inner turmoil, and the months of loneliness, it was as though she'd walked out of a cave into the light of day.

"What's it like to be loved like that?" she asked.

He gave her a quick, questioning glance. Even set in lines of consternation, his features were handsome—a broad brow, nicely arched eyebrows over calm dark eyes. But when he assumed the role of one of his villains, those eyes could express such a range of emotion, such bristling energy, such dark, forbidden thoughts.

His nose was Hollywood-perfect, strong and straight; his mouth was wide and expressive with beautiful white teeth; and his chin had a captivating cleft in it that made him deadly gorgeous in close-ups.

In a suit, he looked as though he had stepped off the cover of *Premiere*.

"Aren't nuns loved like that?" he asked. "I thought children were always flocking around them, and adults were always going to them for advice."

"Yes…but a respect for the habit keeps them at a certain emotional distance." She smiled. "People seem to relate to you as though you represent something in them. I wonder how many villains have attracted the kind of interest people show in you."

He seemed surprised by that observation. "Then you've watched a lot of movies."

"Of course," she replied. "Nuns are people, too. We like love stories, and mysteries, and high adventure. I even like horror movies."

He laughed. She liked the sound.

"Nothing's more fun than a box of popcorn and an old Vincent Price movie. Now *there* was a villain."

Duncan drove the slow speed limit through downtown Dancer's Beach, keeping his sun visor down in an attempt, she guessed, to avoid detection by his ardent fans.

They passed old board-and-batten buildings from early in the century interspersed with post-war store fronts and several modern fast-food franchises. Streetlights were hung with flower baskets, and every block boasted a bench for sitting and watching the world go by. She found the town a wonderful place.

"Did the wedding go well?" she asked, trying to make polite conversation.

He smiled as he watched the road. "Very well. It was just family and our next-door neighbors, but that alone makes sixteen people."

"My goodness. With or without the babies?"

"Without." He picked up speed as he left the four-block main street behind.

"Dori said you just got back from Africa."

"Just a couple of days ago. I was looking forward to a few weeks off with nothing to do but garden. Then I discovered I had twins."

She remained quiet for a moment, unsure what to say. "I don't imagine two babies would leave much time for planting roses."

"I have orders to plant roses under my parents' bedroom window," he said, giving her a surprised glance. "How did you know that?"

"I didn't," she replied. "We just passed a broken-down picket fence with wild roses climbing all over it, and it looked so picturesque. Dori told me that you and your brothers have this wonderful old house, and…I guess I was just picturing roses in my mind."

He nodded. "Logical. Dori's also arguing for window boxes in the front."

"Mmm," she agreed, "with nasturtiums hanging over. Pink ones."

He cast her another interested glance. "You like to garden?"

She shrugged a shoulder. "I like flowers, but I've never had my own space."

"Ah. Convent living."

"I'd love to grow vegetables, too. Carrots and green peppers and tomatoes, and a whole patch of pumpkins."

"You should have entered a farming order of nuns," he teased.

She laughed, feeling herself relax.

"Where's your family?" he asked.

Her laughter fled and tension reclaimed its hold on her. She fought it. "Oh," she replied airily, "just doing their own thing. They travel a lot and we don't see each other very much."

"I'm sorry," he said with sincerity. "Starting over must be difficult all alone."

She shrugged. "It'll be easier now that I have a job. And babies are more than a job, aren't they? They're a purpose—a vocation in themselves."

He took his eyes from the road quickly to smile at her. "That kind of talk will earn you a raise before you even start."

She grinned. "That's nice to know. I'm saving for a car."

He turned off the highway and up a quiet street. "We're going to have to do something about transportation right away," he laughed. "I don't have a car, either. My brother lent me this one."

She ran a hand over the white leather interior of the seats. "I suppose you're used to cabs and limos."

He nodded. "I am driven around a lot. I think I'll get an old pickup like Dillon's so I can get around anonymously."

"That would only work if you never got out of the truck."

"True," he admitted grudgingly.

He slowed down and pulled into the driveway of a

large white two-story house. Ariel fell in love with it immediately. After the sameness of many southern California development homes and the pseudo-Victorians going up everywhere, this was the real thing: center-gabled first and second levels, a wrap-around porch on one side with carved railings and tall columns at about ten-foot intervals, trim and shutters painted a cozy green.

As she watched, a man about Duncan's age, in suit pants and a white shirt and tie, dribbled a basketball toward a fruit basket nailed above the garage door. A young boy and an older man, also in what looked like Sunday best, guarded his progress to the basket. The man made elaborate and comical tosses from one hand to the other in a clear attempt to confuse them.

The boy finally leapt at his middle with a warrior-like cry and, as the man abandoned the ball in an attempt to brace the boy's weight, the older man captured the ball, tossed it cleanly, and dunked it.

The three laughed uproariously.

Ariel turned to Duncan to find him smiling fondly at the trio. "My brother, my nephew, and my father," he said, pushing his door open. He walked around to help her out. "Come on, I'll introduce you. Don't worry about your bag, I'll get it later."

There must have been a full twenty minutes of introductions. After meeting the basketball players, Ariel followed Duncan inside and was introduced to small groups of family members as they moved through the house.

There were aunts in the living room, parents and a sister-in-law in the kitchen, neighbors leaving with covered bowls of food.

In the upstairs hallway, they encountered the new-lyweds in one of the bedrooms, packing.

"I thought you guys weren't leaving until morning with the aunts," Duncan said.

Dillon confirmed that with a nod. He held a little boy about a year old, whom he introduced as Darian. "But we thought since Ariel will probably be using our room—it's most convenient to yours and the babies—we'll vacate tonight and sleep downstairs on the sofa bed."

Duncan shook his head. "Your wedding night on a sofa sleeper within yards of your parents' bedroom? I don't think so. I'm going to let her have my room for tonight, and I'll sleep on the sofa."

"Wait." Ariel raised a hand to quell the argument. "I really appreciate your democratic attitudes, but I'm the hired help. *I'll* take the sofa."

When Duncan opened his mouth to insist, she cleared her throat and explained with a little embarrassment, "I'm a restless sleeper anyway, and until I learn the lay of the house, I won't disturb anyone if I get up to move around. The ground floor's probably the best place for me. And I'll manage to stay out of the way until everyone's gone to bed."

Duncan considered her a moment, then finally nodded. "All right. But you don't have to hide out. Everybody's leaving early in the morning, so I don't think we'll have our usual midnight movie marathons." He patted Dillon's shoulder and kissed Harper's cheek. "Thanks anyway for the offer."

"We were just trying to be nice," Dillon said with a smile at Ariel. "After all, she's going to have to put up with you for the next few weeks." His expression turned suddenly grave. "How *do* you intend to cope?"

The McKeons were a cheerful group who seemed to express their affection for one other with continuous teasing, Ariel decided. She found their attitude contagious, and mimicked Dillon's expression. "I'll be fine. I'm used to a life of self-sacrifice."

Dillon laughed, then nodded approvingly. "Well, Dunk, now I can leave you with the knowledge that in my absence, someone else will bedevil you with skill and style. Thank you, Ariel."

She nodded soberly. "Of course."

Harper, she noticed, was studying her quietly while the men harangued each other. Ariel met her questioning look with one of her own. Harper finally looked away.

"Come on—" Duncan drew Ariel toward a half-opened door across the hall "—I'll introduce you to the babies. They're much nicer than their uncle."

INSIDE THE ivory-colored room with large, carved oak furniture, Duncan pointed toward the portable crib near the window.

He'd done the right thing, he decided as the nanny leaned into the crib and expelled a heartfelt "Oh!" of appreciation for what she, too, seemed to consider two of the most beautiful babies in the world.

Her gentle face softened perceptibly and her hands hovered over the twins as though she would touch them. Then she seemed to change her mind and drew her hands back.

"Look at their little hands!" she whispered, pointing to the tiny fingers linked together in sleep.

That had touched him, too, the first time he'd seen it. It was as though the baby girls were already allied for a lifetime. In the absence of their mother and the confusion over their father, they clung to each other for love and support.

Ariel apparently changed her mind again and touched a fingertip to each little cheek. "They're so beautiful," she whispered. "And so identical!" Then her hand went to Michelle's tiny red fingertip and she looked up at him worriedly. Her eyes were wide. "What is that?" she asked.

He leaned beside her into the crib. "It's called Skin Scribe. Doctors use it to mark the skin for radiation treatments and that kind of thing. In this case they used it just so Darrick could tell one baby from the other when he brought them home from the hospital and took the bracelets off. We've just kept using it. That's Michelle."

She put a fingertip to the little pleat on the baby's brow and one tight little fist. "She looks a little more tense than the other," she observed.

Surprised that she'd seen that so quickly, Duncan congratulated himself on having taken Dori's advice in hiring her. Ariel might not have much experience with babies, but she seemed to be intuitive.

"She is," he said. "Gabrielle's quieter. Eats more. But they're both sleeping eight to ten hours most nights now, and fussing a lot less during the day, according to my brothers." He straightened away from the crib and grinned. "Dillon and Darrick are clearly resentful that I missed the every-two-hour feedings and the mystery screeches that drive you to madness."

She touched each baby one more time, as if she couldn't resist, then straightened and smiled.

Her smile had a new quality, he thought. Perhaps she'd decided she was going to like it here. That was good. Now he wouldn't have to worry about the twins while he went in search of their mother.

"Come on," he said. "We'll get you something to eat, I'll get your bag, and we'll—" He didn't get to finish. Dori appeared in the bedroom doorway and Ariel flew at her like a smart bomb at a target.

They whispered excitedly, arm in arm, as they went into the hallway. "How have you been?" "How's the thesis coming?" "Don't you think they're the most beautiful babies?" "How's...?"

Duncan tried to sidle past them as they laughed and talked, but Dori caught his arm before he could head for the stairs. "Can I borrow Ariel for a few minutes?" she asked. "I want to show her what you've done with my attic. And I want to introduce her to Olivia."

Duncan shook his head tolerantly. "Darrick and Dillon told me about that. I can't believe that a woman about to get her master's degree thinks a ghost visits the attic."

"I'm not saying she visits," Dori corrected him, an angle to her chin. "I just think she left the bodice."

"The what?" Ariel asked.

Dori shushed her with a wave of her hand. "I'll show you." Then, as though to validate her position, she said righteously, "Skye believes in her. And Harper does, too."

"They're married to our brothers," Duncan pointed out. "You have to make allowances for warped viewpoints and mental stress. There are no ghosts."

Dori folded her arms. "Then how did you manage to play a vampire so convincingly?"

"Money," he replied, "and a bad attitude because my bat wings pinched." He rolled his eyes at Ariel.

"I know Dori's your friend, but remember that she's also a little nuts." When Dori gasped, he went on placatingly, "It's part of your charm and I love you for it, but it makes you a little shaky as a dependable source of information. You guys coming down for dinner or do you want me to bring something up to you?"

Dori socked him in the arm. "We'll be down."

Ariel followed Dori up a fold-down ladder that led into an attic room running the length of the house. The walls were rough and unfinished, and a rustic bed and dresser decorated the room along with a slightly ratty but comfortable-looking love seat. A bright rug on the floor lent color, and a small bathroom that smelled of fresh paint had been built in one corner.

Dori spread both arms as she turned slowly in a circle. "Isn't this just the greatest place? Dillon fixed it up for me."

Ariel followed her circuit and was agreeing heartily when she realized they weren't alone. Two women sat casually on the big quilt-covered bed. Skye, the dark-haired sister-in-law she'd met in the kitchen, was propped against the pillows; Harper, the little blonde who'd just married Dillon and who'd stared at her when Duncan had introduced them, sat cross-legged near one of the footposts.

Both of them stared at her intently.

Ariel smiled as she maintained her position several feet away. "Hello, again," she said.

"Again, indeed," Skye frowned. "Hello at last is more like it!"

"What do you mean?" Ariel asked.

"We know," Harper said.

Ariel studied her in puzzlement. "Know what?"

Harper pointed to her. "That you're the babies' mother," Harper said.

Chapter Four

Ariel stared at Skye and Harper. "I beg your pardon?" she said.

They stared back at her. "You're the babies' mother, aren't you?" Harper spoke, and the question definitely had the air of an accusation.

Ariel turned to Dori in confusion, then back to Harper. "I'm the nanny, remember? Duncan just intro—"

Skye waved away the rest of her denial. "We know. That's what *he* thinks. But you're her, aren't you? The one he made love to that night above the cantina?"

Dori put an arm around Ariel's shoulders. "You'll have to forgive them," she said, shaking her head at her sisters-in-law. "There's quite a mystery surrounding the twins' mother, Ariel. And these two have let their imaginations go a little crazy."

"You said the babies' mother was a friend of yours," Harper reminded Dori. "Ariel is a friend of yours."

Dori rolled her eyes. "You think I have only one?"

Skye sighed, her brow furrowing. "There are moments when I'd be surprised you even had *one*."

"Thank you," Dori said gravely. "I love you, too."

"She's the right height and weight," Skye argued,

"according to the medical records at Valley Memorial."

Harper rose off the bed and came to study Ariel. "The nurses said she had long dark hair." She spoke distractedly as she walked slowly around Ariel.

Dori remained protectively close.

"Hair can be cut." Skye also rose and leaned against the post at the foot of the bed. "And one of the nurses said she was quite pretty."

"Well, there you have it," Ariel said lightly. "That leaves me out altogether."

Harper stopped in front of her and looked her over feature by feature. "You're not glamorous," she finally declared, "but only because you've made no effort to be. No makeup, short hair, careless clothes…"

"Harper!" Dori protested. "Honestly. She's just two months out of the convent with no money. You're being awful!"

Harper stood her ground another moment, then seemed to relax a little. She folded her arms and her expression became uncertain. "All right, I apologize. I'm not sure, so I shouldn't be making accusations. But your friend Julietta has put us all through quite a lot. While we understand why she had to leave the babies, and even why she had to hide. I'm not sure I'll ever understand putting one brother after the other through the ordeal of thinking he was the babies' father and then learning he wasn't."

There was a brief silence, then Dori squeezed Ariel's shoulders. "My brothers are really very nice," she said with a condemning glance at Skye and Harper. "They just seem to have chosen these warrior women who've grown very protective of them and the twins."

Ariel nodded, smiling at Harper and Skye. "I can't find fault with that. My family's all over the place and we don't get to see much of each other, but they're still very important to me. I wouldn't let anyone hurt them as long as I draw breath. So, please don't worry. I promise to continue keeping the babies safe until this… What's her name?''

"Julietta,'' Dori provided.

"Until Julietta can come home to them. All right?''

Skye and Harper looked her over one more time, exchanged glances, then smiled. "All right,'' Harper said. "Again, I apologize.''

"That's not necessary,'' Ariel assured her.

"And just to show you that we trust you…'' Skye took her arm and drew her toward an antique dress form standing before a cheval glass. On the form was a beautifully beaded top and plain silk skirt of what appeared to be a wedding dress. "We're going to introduce you to Olivia's legacy.''

Ariel couldn't quite believe her eyes. The top of the dress was absolutely exquisite. It had a ruffled band collar, and pearl and bugle beads in the shape of a V from shoulder to waist. Beads also decorated the pointed hems of the long sleeves. The silk skirt had simply been pinned to the top.

"Who does it belong to?'' Ariel asked.

"I think it belongs to us,'' Skye replied, taking the pointed end of a sleeve and holding it as though affectionately touching the hand of whoever had once worn the dress.

"I don't understand.'' Ariel leaned closer to study the beading.

"It was just left here, so we're not sure. And we don't know when or by whom.''

"According to Dori's brothers," Harper added, "it wasn't here when they bought the house in February. And the Realtor says it wasn't here when she arranged for the house painter. She had to come into the attic to open the windows so they could anchor their scaffolding to paint the gables."

"But it *was* here—" Skye picked up the story "—when Darrick and I arrived with the babies in May. I climbed just high enough up the ladder to be able to look into the attic—and there were the form and the mirror. Darrick insists he had never seen them before."

"So, how," Ariel asked practically, "did it get here?"

Her three companions exchanged a look, then Skye assumed a vaguely defensive stance. "We think Olivia Marbury left it for us."

"A friend? A neighbor?"

Harper shook her head. "Actually, she's a woman who's been dead for at least fifty years."

Ariel focused on Harper, trying to make sense of her words. "Dead," she repeated, looking from one woman to the next, waiting for one of them to correct her. No one did.

In fact, they nodded.

She smiled hesitantly. "This is some kind of hazing ritual, right? Because you think I'm this Julietta person, and you hate me?"

Frowning, Harper crossed her ankles and folded gracefully to the bright carpet in front of the dress form. She caught Ariel's wrist and pulled her down with her. Dori and Skye joined them.

"We don't hate Julietta," she corrected. "In fact, we've kept Dori's secret about her from the men because we know she had to do what she did to protect her father and her babies and the man she loved.''

''You mean…Duncan?''

''Yes. But about Olivia—''

''You have to start at the beginning,'' Skye interrupted. ''Unless she understands how Dancer's Beach came to be, she won't get the whole thing.''

''Wait.'' Ariel eyed the dress warily. ''Is it really critical that I understand this? I mean…if we're talking—'' she had to force the word out ''—*ghosts*, I don't think I want to know any more. That's not really a subject I'm comfortable with, you know? I mean…''

Skye smiled with understanding. ''It's a startling notion for anyone.''

''But if she's going to be here,'' Harper insisted, ''she has to understand.''

Skye nodded. ''But having been a nun, she probably believes in spirituality, but not the paranormal. Right, Ariel?''

''No,'' Ariel replied. Three pairs of eyes studied her more closely, waiting for an explanation. ''I don't like the subject of ghosts because once I…'' She hesitated because she'd never shared this with anyone but her father, and he'd insisted she was mistaken. ''I think I saw my mother…after she died.''

The room went still. Ariel felt the air constrict around her. For a moment she felt as though the admission would choke her. Then her companions, two of them little more than strangers, leaned toward her commiseratingly and encouraged her to go on. She drew in a deep gulp of air.

The sudden freedom of having admitted her secret, of having someone else apparently *believe* her, gave her the courage to go on.

"My father was sure I'd imagined it," she told them, warming to her story as they leaned closer. "That I was thinking of her so much in my adolescence because all the other girls had mothers but me. She died when I was six." She shook her head, remembering the plump, smiling, dark-haired woman. "But I *know* I saw her. I was walking to school, and my brothers had run ahead to be with their friends. I was twelve, and very lonely and confused about our...about everything. Then suddenly she was walking beside me and she told me not to worry, that everything would be fine, that I would grow up to find great happiness."

"Wow," Harper said softly. "*My* mother died when I was a teenager. There were moments when I'd have given anything to be able to see her again."

Ariel nodded, understanding that feeling. "And after that, I seemed to be able to get it together. To move on and try to find my place. But my father didn't like me to talk about the incident, so I didn't. I think he missed her too much to hear it."

"Maybe," Dori suggested, "he was a little jealous that she hadn't 'visited' him."

"Maybe." Ariel sat a little straighter. She sighed and looked up at the beautiful dress with its pinned skirt. "So one way or another, it seems I'm destined to deal with people...that not everyone sees. Tell me the story. You said it starts with how Dancer's Beach came to be?"

"Right—" Skye picked up the tale "—four dancers from San Francisco were headed for the gold fields in the Klondike in 1898 when the ship they were on floundered on the rocks right off the coast here."

Ariel had begun to imagine the ghost of a woman

who'd drowned at sea, but Skye's smile suggested that that episode hadn't ended in tragedy.

"Three brothers named Buckley had started a small sawmill here. The oldest, Barton, was on top of the hill behind us, checking it out as a place to build a house. He saw the wreck and gathered his brothers and some friends—and they managed to save everyone."

"And they married the dancers!" Harper said with a pleased grin. "Don't you love it? Don't you wish you could write romance? What a great story." Then she sobered. "Of course, there were four dancers and only three brothers. Olivia was almost thirty, the oldest of the dancers, and she fell in love with Barton. But she wasn't in very good health, and he wanted a big family like the one he came from. So he married India Winfield, the youngest of the group. She's described as 'robust' in some family letters."

"What did Olivia do?" Ariel asked.

"Went on to the Klondike," Skye replied. Then she reached out to finger the hem of the skirt. "When I found this, it was just the bodice on the form, as though someone had started it, then had to change plans suddenly. I think Olivia thought she'd be marrying Barton, started the dress, then maybe abandoned it when she went to the Klondike."

"So...this is the house Barton built?" She pointed to the floor on which they all sat.

"No," Dori answered. "This is the house he built for his son. But Skye did some research and found that Olivia came back here in her old age and stayed with Barton's son and daughter-in-law. At least we *think* it was Olivia. The daughter-in-law wrote a cookbook, and she mentions a recipe provided by her old aunt who was staying with them."

"But would Olivia be her aunt if she didn't marry Barton?"

Skye nodded. "We have two theories on that. Family friends are often called aunt and uncle even if they aren't by blood."

"That's true."

"Or—" she paused dramatically and grinned "—and we really like this one better—Barton eventually went to the Klondike to find Olivia when India died twelve years after they were married. And she finally had reason to finish the dress."

"You mean he went after her?" Ariel was surprised to find herself pleased by that possibility. She was captivated by their story: a woman in love, whose love wasn't returned and who chose to make her life elsewhere when she knew it would be painful to see the man she loved with someone else.

"He *did* book passage to Canada. Harper talked to the manager of the hotel downtown, who is also a Buckley family enthusiast because the hotel was owned by Matthew and Alice Buckley, the third brother and his wife. She had an old rolltop desk that belonged to Alice, and she found, slipped behind one of the drawers, a photo of Barton with a woman who *isn't* India. Can you go get those, Harper?"

"Sure." Harper got to her feet and disappeared down the ladder to the second floor.

Skye continued, "We haven't identified the woman in the photo, but we like to think it's Olivia. Aunt Gracie and Aunt Edith have friends in Canada who are checking the historical society for Olivia's and Barton's names to see if we can place them there."

A small detail bothered Ariel. "But you said when

Skye first saw the dress, it *didn't* have a skirt. So what makes you think she finished it?''

Dori laughed. ''Cussedness. We want this to have a happy ending.''

''And this.'' Harper emerged through the attic's trap door, two photos held aloft. She handed them to Ariel.

In the first photo a handsome man in turn-of-the century dress clothes and a mustache posed with a lovely, slightly startled-looking, fair-haired woman. He wore a top hat; she a slim-waisted ball gown. There was a plume in her hair.

''This is Olivia?'' Ariel looked into the eyes of the woman and saw sadness and joy behind the soft surprise.

''That's what we think,'' Harper replied. ''And the other photo's obviously a christening.''

Ariel put the second photo atop the first and saw a different man and woman. In the woman's arms was a baby in a long, traditional baptismal dress.

''Look closely at the christening dress,'' Skye said.

Ariel brought the photo closer to her face to study the obscure detail. Then she saw it—the barely visible network of lines that suggested a pattern. Beading, she guessed. Then she recognized the V-shape, just like the beading on the bodice of the wedding dress.

She looked up at her companions, her mouth agape. ''The christening dress…was made out of the skirt of the wedding dress!''

Skye clapped her hands. ''Right! So we think it means Barton found Olivia, she finished the dress, they got married, and that's *their* baby.''

Ariel frowned at the photo. ''But this couple isn't them.''

''Godparents?'' Harper suggested.

Ariel was now completely bewitched by their theory. "What happens next?" she asked.

Harper reclaimed the photos. "We wait for word
from my aunt's friends in Canada. Meanwhile, Skye
and I will keep researching what we can while Dori's
studying in Nova Scotia." She smiled at Ariel. "But
you're the one who's going to be here, so take care
of the dress, okay?"

Ariel looked up at it again. It fairly glowed in the
shaft of light from the attic window. "But…why do
you think she *left* it? I mean, don't ghosts communi-
cate with this world because of something unresolved
in their lives? I mean—I want to believe she married
Barton and had the baby, too, but if she did—then
nothing's unresolved."

Skye nodded thoughtfully. "I think she's just tied
to this house, maybe. And the dress was kind of a gift
to us."

"The babies brought Darrick and me together, but
the dress played an important part in our finally being
able to *be* together."

"And it helped Dillon and me," Harper said.
"We'd been together and broken up, and just couldn't
understand each other. But the twins forced us together
and the dress helped us figure out what we meant to
each other."

"So, its work is done?"

Skye shook her head. "I don't think so, because
none of us has been able to wear it yet. I'm too tall,
Harper's too short. Maybe Duncan's woman will be
just right."

Ariel stared, then smiled. "It's a nice idea. Then all
the McKeon brothers will be happily married. But how
does that solve Olivia's issues, whatever they are?"

Skye shook her head. "I don't know. We'll just have to wait and see."

Ariel looked a little nervously at the dress. "Olivia doesn't...visit, does she? It was one thing to be calm with the spirit of my mother, but I'm not sure how I'd deal with the ghost of a total stranger."

"Well, there you have it," Harper said, unfolding to stand. "Olivia's not a stranger. She brought us a gift. And husbands. That makes her a friend."

"But relax." Skye patted Ariel's arm. "So far Olivia hasn't put in an actual appearance. We've just sort of...felt she was here."

Ariel tried to be reassured by that as a loud rap sounded on the trap door. "Dinner, ladies!" a male voice called.

Harper went to pull open the door, and Dillon rose head and shoulders into the room. He frowned at the little circle the other three women made around the dress form.

"You're not trying to call her up or anything, are you?" he asked worriedly. "I don't think there's an inch of room left at the dinner table."

Harper patted his head. "Nothing like that. We were just talking. We'll be right down. What's for dinner?"

"Major leftovers," he said. "Everything from the brot-and-beer fest we had yesterday to the rest of the wedding buffet." He grinned up at her. "Are you still thrilled that you married me?"

He rose a rung higher on the ladder, and Harper leaned down to kiss him. "Ecstatic," she replied. "Now get out of my way so I can get to the food."

Dinner reminded Ariel of a minor riot, albeit a cheerful one. The noise level was deafening, all manner of food seemed to be flying past her, and the en-

thusiasm of the participants occasionally made her feel
her life was in danger.

The energy was high, the goodwill powerful, the joy
almost palpable. She was filled with admiration one
moment and jealousy the next.

Her family had been like this when her mother was
alive. But that had been so long ago that she could
hardly think that far back.

Besides, she was here to start over, not to look back.

The babies lay on a blanket on the floor, and Duncan, who sat at the end of the table, leaned down every
once in a while to retrieve Michelle, whose constant
flailing propelled her onto the carpet.

When dinner was over, everyone joined in cleanup,
while Dillon helped Duncan feed the babies.

"Shouldn't I do that?" Ariel asked Dillon while the
sounds of running water, clattering dishes and laughter
came from the kitchen.

Dillon shook his head as he settled comfortably into
a corner of the sofa. "No. You're not on duty until
tomorrow. Anyway, this is my last chance to do this
for a while, and I'm going to miss it."

"Why don't you and Dori take a walk along the
beach?" Duncan suggested, stretched out in the other
corner. "You two haven't had much chance to catch
up."

Dori, walking by with an armful of dishes, cheered
the idea. "Excellent thought," she said, smiling at Ariel. "I'll meet you on the front porch in a few
minutes."

When Dori shrugged into a jacket a while later and
headed for the front door, Dillon called after her. "Ariel seems like a nice quiet girl. Please don't corrupt
her with your bad habits."

Dori stopped, her hand on the doorknob. "I'm the youngest sibling. Where would I have gotten *my* bad habits, do you suppose?"

"From the brother just older than you," Duncan answered seriously. "The one you'd have spent the most time with."

Dillon frowned at him. "She'd have gotten them from the oldest sibling who was *supposed* to have set a good example, but instead paid us a measly fifty cents to deliver your paper route, taught us to skip the step that creaked when sneaking downstairs after lights-out, *and* to get into the Friday-night football games free if we climbed the ash tree at the edge of the parking lot and fell onto the top seat of the bleachers."

"Those aren't bad habits, they're important life lessons," countered Duncan. "Her bad habits must have come from the middle child. Everybody knows how screwed up middle children are."

"I beg your pardon." Darrick, gathering up the tablecloth for the laundry, abandoned the task and came to stand behind the sofa. "On the chance that you hadn't noticed, Einstein, I'm the second child whether or not you count Donovan in the number."

Duncan granted that with a nod. "But after Donovan died and before Dori, it was just the three of us for quite a while. Hey—" he forestalled Darrick's further protest with a shrug of his shoulders, his hands occupied with the baby and the bottle "—I'm just trying to come up with some reasonable explanation for you."

"The reasonable explanation for me," Darrick said, "is that I followed you, then had to put up with all the younger ones because you were busy being Mr. Great.''

Duncan grinned. ''I wasn't busy at it at all. It came very naturally. Something you've always been jealous of.''

Darrick made a scornful sound. ''You're lucky you're holding a baby.''

Dori pulled the door open. ''You know what the really sad thing is about this whole discussion?'' she demanded.

''What?'' Duncan and his brothers asked simultaneously.

She angled her chin. ''That you should be praising each other instead of trying to plant the blame—because there *is* nothing wrong with me.'' And she swept out the door, hoots of dissension following her.

ARIEL LAY IN the darkened living room hours later, the house finally quiet after a good hour of settling-down noises, quiet conversations, and good-nights called across hallways.

She briefly considered her past, which had been alternately wonderful and very frightening, and she thought about her family, whom she hadn't seen in some time. She felt the sting of tears in her eyes as she realized how much she missed them. It was the loud good cheer of the McKeons, she guessed, that made the night so dark and quiet in contrast, that made her so jealously aware of how rich they were in their love and pleasure in one another.

Tomorrow my life starts anew, she told herself bracingly, snuggling into her pillow. *In the morning, the family will be gone and it'll just be Duncan McKeon and the twins and me.* Then she remembered the crowd at the airport and conceded with a dry smile into the darkness, *And every fan Duncan has in Dancer's Beach.*

But that was all right. She could work around them. It was important to her future that she be a brilliant nanny. And she would be.

She would be up early in the morning—before everyone else. She would make the coffee and have her blankets folded and her bed made so that no one could think of her as an intruder.

Her job was to remain in the background, to be vigilant, to anticipate needs and fill them.

Though Duncan McKeon was a very new father, he looked as though he intended to be very hands-on in his role.

This was going to be tricky.

Very tricky.

Chapter Five

Duncan and Ariel, each holding a twin, waved at the departing caravan of cars. The day was bright and warm, and the sun gleamed off the high roof of Charlie and Peg's camper, bringing up the rear, until it finally disappeared around a bend in the road.

"When will they be back?" Ariel asked, bumping foreheads with Michelle in her arms. The baby smiled broadly and kicked both arms and legs.

"Dori's birthday is early in August," he said, walking to the garage and pulling up the door. He took several steps inside, and finished absently, "I imagine everyone'll be back for that. Then I'm due in Maui."

Uncertain whether to follow him into the garage, she stood just outside on the driveway. The garage was crowded with odds and ends of furniture, paint cans, leftover wallboard and pipe. "They're filming a movie remake about King Arthur on Maui?" she asked in surprise. Dori had filled her in on the Spielberg project.

He turned at that, laughing lightly. "No. I'm not doing Arthur. A friend of mine is preparing a documentary on Lahaina's history as a whaling port, and asked me to narrate."

"Ah. A business-pleasure kind of job."

"Right." He looked up at the rafters where lengths of lumber and odd pieces of wood were stored. "I guess there'll be room to fit one car in here. The other will have to sit outside."

"You're going to buy *two* cars?" Ariel shifted Michelle to her other hip.

"You'll need something to get around in," he said.

"But can't we just share one? I'm a good driver. And I'll probably only use it to run errands and go for groceries. And only if it rains. Town is just a good walk away. It'd be wasteful to buy two cars."

He smiled at her insistence. "I know nuns take a vow of poverty, but actors take one of abundance. And anyway, I was just going to pick up a couple of used cars."

"One good used car would serve us very well," she pressed.

"It'll all depend on what we can find anyway." He pulled the garage door closed again and led the way to the house. "I'm going to make a few phone calls. If you'll do a groceries inventory while I'm doing that, we'll pack up the babies when I'm finished and head to town to see what we can find."

"Of course."

AN HOUR LATER, Duncan frowned at the notes he'd scribbled on a napkin. Jeanine Curry, the camera-woman who'd shared his table that fateful night in Puerta Flora, was working in Toronto and wouldn't be back in the States for at least a week. Yvette Dela-croix, his co-star on the film, was at work in the Gobi Desert on some high-adventure project with Stallone.

And his agent's secretary had no idea where Phoebe

Price was. "She came back from lunch at the Bel Air Hotel," Quenby said, "collected her messages, said something about setting the heathen straight once and for all, and ran out of here like her tail was on fire."

"You mean it was just another day?" he'd asked drily.

She'd laughed. "Except that she was angry."

"She's always angry."

"No," Quenby had corrected, "she's always the-atrically furious. That's a different thing, filled with the electricity of the moment. This was a deep-down thing. She was *angry*."

"Okay." He sighed. His hopes of taking a step to-ward resolving the mystery of his babies' parentage were well and truly dashed, at least for the time being. "If she shorts out or something and comes back to recharge, have her call me."

"You got it."

Accepting that he was going to have to wait before he could even hope for a clue about where his life was going, Duncan pocketed the napkin and went in search of Ariel.

He found her reciting her grocery list to the babies while she secured them in their double-width, brightly upholstered carriage. As he came up behind her, un-detected, he saw the twins watching her in complete fascination.

Duncan also noticed the lovely line of her backside as she leaned into the carriage, then felt instantly ashamed of himself for the observation. The woman had been a nun, after all. And while it was true that she'd left the convent, she probably hadn't abandoned the spiritual tenets that had led her there in the first place. She wouldn't appreciate his leering.

"Pasta," she said in a voice appropriate to the discovery of gold, "spaghetti sauce, Italian sausage, French bread, garlic, salad greens, red and yellow peppers, a shaker of those crunchy things you put on top of salad." She tucked blankets in and adjusted the carriage's bonnet halfway back to shield the infants from the glare of the sun while still allowing it to warm them.

"Our cook was weight-conscious and never made spaghetti," she explained to the babies. "Or anything else really good. She was big on skinned chicken breasts and baked fish. Now I want beans, hot dogs, hamburgers with the works, and that includes ranch dressing for the French fries. Onion rings, ribs and barbecue sauce..." Then she closed her eyes and leaned over them to whisper in a sort of trance induced by the recitation of foods, "Biscuits and *gravy!*"

Both babies made high-pitched noises of delight at her closeness and kicked under the blanket.

Duncan bit back laughter, imagining some dragon of an older nun probably watching her sugar and cholesterol levels and imposing all her restrictions on the convent for which she cooked.

"And guess what we're going to get for you?" she asked the babies.

They waited as though they'd understood the question and anticipated the answer.

"Cereal!" she said with a "ta-da" spread of her arms. "Your Aunt Harper says you, Gabrielle, tried to eat the bottle the last time she fed you, so she thinks you're ready for bigger stuff. Well, so am I. I hope your dad isn't too much of a health-food freak. Of course, I'm sure he didn't get that body by being careless."

Duncan felt a moment of pleased surprise. His well-muscled physique was almost as necessary a tool to his career as was his talent. Taking care of it had become second nature. He was accustomed to fan magazines mentioning his washboard abs or his well-defined pecs, but this compliment had come from a woman conditioned to ignore the physical.

He felt slightly off balance that she'd noticed. And far less guilty about his nice-*derrière* observation.

"I exercise a lot," he said, interrupting her listing of desserts. She straightened and turned with a start, her cheeks flushing with color. He delicately ignored it. "I can eat anything without gaining an ounce. But I usually forego desserts." He picked up the carriage and walked down the porch steps with it, setting it on the walk. Then he pulled sunglasses out of his back pocket and put on a baseball cap, setting the visor low over his eyes. "All set to go?"

She opened her mouth, and he thought for a moment that she was going to apologize for the remark, or at least explain. But she seemed to decide that it would be better to ignore it. "I just have to run in and get the diaper bag and my purse."

She was back in a minute with what looked like enough gear to supply an expedition. She tucked the diaper bag onto the rack on the bottom of the carriage and slung a large straw purse over her shoulder.

When she started to push the carriage, he brushed her aside. "I'll push," he said, and headed out.

She caught up with him at the driveway and stayed abreast. "*I'm* the nanny. *I'm* supposed to push."

"I'm the dad," he countered, "and everybody else has been doing my work for a couple of months. And doing it very well, it seems. Aren't these the healthiest looking, most beautiful babies you've ever seen?''

"Yes, they are," she had to agree. "The world would be a much saner place if all babies were loved by so many people. But I'm going to have to earn my salary.''

He nodded. "Darrick and Dillon assure me that these two generate enough physical and emotional work for four people, so don't worry. And if you act like a companion rather than a nanny, maybe people won't recognize me and we'll have some peace on this walk.''

"I seriously doubt that," Ariel said. But she was happy to walk beside him into the warm July morning. The air smelled of sunshine and wildflowers and the fragrant mysteries of the ocean.

Dancer's Beach had apparently not yet been discovered by vacationers because houses were on large lots, there were no apartments, only one motel, and no beachfront crowding. Though she and Duncan had now reached the main highway through town, traffic was light, but those who did pass, she noticed, gawked. Duncan's hat and sunglasses weren't fooling anybody.

The babies earned a greeting and an interested peek into their carriage from a pair of old men sitting side by side, working a crossword puzzle together on one of the street-side benches.

Ariel noticed the Buckley Arms, a five-story, gray-and-white hotel. She remembered Skye telling her that one of the Buckley brothers had been an hotelier.

"Where's the car dealership?" Ariel asked. "I didn't notice one when you drove me home from the airport.''

Duncan pointed ahead of them. "It's a couple of blocks up, then a block over. They deal only in used cars but they'll have something to keep us mobile."

"Just one," she said, picking up the earlier argument.

He pulled the carriage to a stop at the only downtown light. "Are nuns allowed to nag?" he teased.

She shook her head. "No. That's why I'm taking full advantage of my freedom now." Then she made a self-deprecating face. "But I suppose nannies aren't allowed to nag, either?"

"Oh, why not?" he asked good-naturedly. The light changed and he started across, Ariel keeping pace. Everyone on the street, she noticed, had turned to stare and point. "As long as you don't mind being ignored, go ahead and take advantage. After we buy some wheels, we'll find you a ribs place or a junk burger."

"You're looking for a truck?" Ariel asked as they turned down the street, headed for the car lot. She could see it now, triangular flags waving, chrome and windshields catching the sunlight.

"I was," he replied, slowing the carriage as an old black Labrador lying in the middle of the sidewalk lifted his head, appeared to consider moving for the strange contraption coming at him, then seemed to decide it was too much trouble.

Duncan laughed and steered carefully around him. "But I did some research last night and discovered that unless a truck has a crew cab, you're not supposed to carry babies in it. They can't ride in the front, and infant seats aren't approved for side-impact in those sideways-facing jump seats. So..." He winced. "I guess I've become the classic station wagon joke—a man in his prime forced to turn away from muscle cars and power trucks in favor of something that'll carry Little League teams safely…or, in my case, ballet troupes.''

"You aren't going to put them in tutus if they really *want* to play Little League, are you?'' she asked.

"Of course not.''

She pointed to Gabrielle, whose arms waved wildly. Michelle seemed to have been sedated by the ride.

"I think Gabrielle's going to have an arm. She might play for the Yankees.''

Duncan stopped at the edge of the curb to check the traffic. A car with a realty company logo emblazoned on the side went by, the driver honking and waving.

Duncan waved back. "Our Realtor,'' he explained to Ariel, then he frowned. "Not the Yankees. The Angels.''

"But the Yankees are a much better team.''

"In New York. That's too far away.''

"But she'll be a baseball star. You'll have to give her her freedom.''

He mulled that over silently, apparently couldn't settle on an argument, and finally said, "You're nagging again.''

She followed him onto the car lot. "You said it was okay,'' she reminded.

"No, NO, NO!'' Duncan had just purchased a garnet 1996 van for himself and was trying to talk Ariel into a beautifully kept four-year-old silver compact station wagon.

The women in the sales office had stared wistfully at Duncan, then giggled like girls when he spoke to them. They pleaded to claim the babies who'd begun fussing the moment the carriage stopped. The women were carrying them around, bouncing them and talking baby talk. Ariel kept track of them out of the corner of her eye.

Duncan had asked the salesman for a few moments of privacy to argue out the issue of the second car. "Don't tell me stubbornness is allowed in the convent," he said, opening the driver's door for her. "Just sit in it."

She shook her head. "I don't *want* to sit in it. Duncan, you cannot pay me a salary *and* buy me an eight-thousand-dollar car. And I can't pay for it."

"Okay, look," he said reasonably, "I told you when we first talked about your being hired that I might have to leave you alone with the twins for a couple of days. I'll be taking the Safari. What if you need something from the store, or some other emergency arises that requires you to get somewhere in a hurry?"

"I'll call a cab."

"Dancer's Beach has only two, and if they're both busy, you're up a creek. Ask Harper. Being unable to get a cab is how she ended up marrying Dillon."

"I believe Dillon can only have one wife in this state, so it's not likely to have the same results for me, is it?"

She saw him fight a grin, then firm his expression.

"If I'm going to leave you alone with my babies, I want to know that you're going to have transportation." He spoke firmly, thinking that the sweet little ex-nun had depths of determination he hadn't suspected.

And while he'd never been one to demand his own way, circumstances had conspired to see that others always gave it to him. And he'd grown used to that.

Her eyelashes flickered. He wondered if that meant she was on the brink of surrender. He also noticed how thick and glossy and dark those lashes were.

He kept talking to distract himself from that observation. "Tell you what. When Dori comes home and takes over again, you leave the car for her."

Her lashes swept down once while she thought, making a captivating crescent-moon pattern on her cheeks.

"The car goes with the position," he went on, wondering what was wrong with him. His life was filled with the world's most stunningly gorgeous women and he seldom noticed that kind of detail. He had to keep talking. "Unless you want to buy it when you leave— then we'll negotiate."

She folded her arms, and her little bosom rose and fell. "All right. Using the car is a perk of the job, but it isn't mine."

"Right."

"Okay."

She was far less reticent when he bought her a burger and fries. The agency needed an hour to wash and put gas in both vehicles, so Duncan took her to a small restaurant with a picnic table and benches set up outside.

"What'll be easier?" Ariel asked. "The stares of the people inside when you walk in, or the passersby begging for your autograph if we sit outside?"

He pointed to a bench around the back and handed her a bill. "Why don't you go in and order two of whatever you want, and I'll stay with the girls. We might get some privacy back here."

Ariel peered into the carriage where both babies were yawning and rubbing their eyes. "They got so much attention at the agency, they're about to drift off to sleep.'' She handed him the bottle of milk from the diaper bag. ''Maybe this'll help.''

Half an hour later, Duncan was very grateful that he'd lost ten pounds filming the last movie. He'd just eaten a bacon burger with cheese, seasoned fries, onion rings, and an ice cream bar.

''Geez.'' He studied the orange-coated treat before taking a bite. ''I can't believe they still make these. I haven't had one of these since—'' he paused to think about it ''—since my parents used to summer at my aunt's on the east coast. We bought these at the food concession at the beach.''

Ariel bit the rounded top of her bar off and nodded while she worked it into a corner of her mouth. ''I'd never seen them until I spent time in Texas. I guess some nostalgia craze brought them back, or made them popular again.''

''Texas?'' he asked around a mouthful of ice cream. ''Your convent was in Texas?''

She sucked hard on the bite of ice cream, waving her hand in front of her mouth to indicate that it was cold. It took her an eternity to answer. And her eyelashes were fluttering. ''No. It was in California. I was in Texas before that.''

''With your parents?''

''With my father. And my brothers.''

''You have family there?''

''Yes.''

She answered amiably but briefly, clearly unwilling to talk about it. That was fine with him. Dori had mentioned that Ariel was relearning the outside world after her time in the convent. Maybe she found it difficult— or troubling. He had to allow for that.

But he didn't like the fact that the smile on her face was in direct counterpoint to the unhappiness in her eyes.

And exactly why he was worried about that, he didn't understand. He had other, bigger problems. Like finding the mother of his babies.

He didn't have time to worry about a look in the eyes of a nanny who'd be gone in another month.

But he worried anyway.

DUNCAN DROVE THE VAN to the supermarket with both babies in the second seat and the carriage folded up in the back. Ariel followed in the small station wagon.

They met over a grocery cart to fill the list she'd made, then added a few frivolities he liked having around: cashews, cheese-jalapeño chips, caramel corn.

Ariel grinned at his contributions. "You're as much of a junk-food junkie as I am."

He nodded. "By the time I go back to work and you go back home, both of us are going to need a fat farm."

She appeared stricken by that suggestion. He was surprised by her reaction and opened his mouth to assure her that he was teasing, when she grinned. "I'll have to run on the beach before the twins are up," she said. "You won't have to worry because you go back to a personal trainer and probably meals tailored to your diet. While I go home to…" She hesitated and the stricken look came back. Then she snatched a jar off the shelf and studied the ingredients. "No point in thinking that far ahead," she said absently as she turned the jar in her hand. "Do we want some of this?"

Duncan watched the top of her dark head as she

perused the label, certain now that Ariel Bonneau wasn't quite as serene inside as she pretended to be on the surface.

And he couldn't help wondering why that was. Or what it had to do with him.

"I don't think," he said, "that we'll need pickled pigs' feet for anything. Unless you have a particular passion for it."

She turned the jar so that she saw the product name, sighed, then replaced the jar on the shelf and moved on without a word.

DUNCAN WAS PULLING INTO the driveway when he noticed a dark-haired woman in a white suit, stockings, and heels sitting on the top step of the porch. She leaned her chin on her hands in an attitude of despondency.

Phoebe.

He felt a firm jolt in his gut. *Dear God,* he prayed, *I like Phoebe. I really do. I'm grateful to you for putting her in my path as an agent. She works hard for me, and together we've built a respected reputation for good work with a minimum of fuss.*

But if it's all the same to You, I'd rather she wasn't the mother of my twins. She's a wonderful agent, Lord, but not what you'd call maternal. And I don't think I could stand being married to her. And I think it'd be better all around if I was married to the mother of my children.

Phoebe rose as he pulled into the garage.

He noticed no cheerful wave as he disappeared into the structure, heard no delighted shout of his name. That meant she was here on business. When business was involved, Phoebe never wasted time on the social amenities.

She followed him into the garage and yanked his door open before he'd even turned off the ignition. "You turned down Steven Spielberg?" she said, her tone a combination of disbelief and horror. "You *turned down* Steven Spielberg?"

He should have known. She stepped back so that he could get out of the car in the narrow space left between it and the lawn tools leaning up against the wall.

He took her by the shoulders and kissed her cheek. That always rattled her. She was tall and formidably built, with generous, though firm curves for a woman in her mid-forties. Her hair was short and dark and styled to take all the softness out of a creamy complexion and round cheeks. She presented a tough-as-nails exterior to her clients and the people in the entertainment industry.

But Duncan knew her. He'd been in her office when her vet had called to tell her that age had overtaken her dachshund and that there was nothing more he could do. Duncan had watched her dissolve into loud sobs. He'd poured her a brandy from the carafe on her Louis XV highboy and taken her in his arms. She'd wept for half an hour. She definitely did have a heart.

"Phoebe, what a lovely surprise." Duncan smiled at her as she shook him off and folded her arms militantly, the gesture intended to blockade herself from any invasive affection.

"Don't turn the charm on me, Deke," she ordered, shaking off the ruffling his kiss on the cheek had caused, and refocusing on him with a fierce expression. "Steven calls me himself to tell me he's just seen *Summer Lovers* and he thinks you're the embodiment of the new millennium's Arthur Pendragon and wants to know where to find you. I prepare to open a Swiss bank account for you to place the millions you're going to amass on a Spielberg project, and *you*—'' she shuddered and closed her eyes, apparently in a paroxysm of outrage ''—you tell him…*no?*''

She picked up a pitchfork leaning against the wall beside her and took a step back to aim it threateningly at him. ''Give me one good reason,'' she said hotly, ''why I shouldn't plunge this into both of us.''

Duncan barely bit back a laugh. He knew that if he succumbed to it, he'd find himself aerated. He thought to himself, not for the first time, that she really was in the wrong end of the business. She'd have made a great actress.

Suddenly his amusement fled when Ariel leapt onto Phoebe's back, screaming and holding the agent tightly around the neck with both arms. The pitchfork clattered to the concrete floor of the garage.

''I've got her!'' she shouted to Duncan. ''Call the police!''

Duncan stared in disbelief—for just a heartbeat—as Phoebe gasped for air and pulled futilely at the arms around her throat. She turned three hundred sixty degrees in her effort to dislodge her attacker, but Ariel rode her as though she were a rearing thoroughbred.

''Ariel, no!'' Half laughing, half shouting, Duncan turned Phoebe so that he could hook an arm around Ariel's waist and extricate her from her prey.

The moment Phoebe was free, she roared with rage and reached for Ariel, who kicked at her with both sneakered feet.

''No! Stop it!'' Duncan put Ariel down and pushed her behind him, grabbing Phoebe's forearms and holding her away. "Listen to me! Ariel, this is my agent, Phoebe Price. She was teasing with the pitchfork. Phoebe, this is my nanny, Ariel Bonneau."

There was a moment of charged silence, then he heard, "Oh, no." He felt Ariel's forehead thunk against his back, heard her voice lower several tones in mortification. "Oh, *no.*"

Phoebe tugged at the hem of her skirt, rebuttoned the front of her jacket, patted her hair. "Nanny?" she asked breathlessly, brushing off her sleeves. "What are you raising? Gorillas?"

"Babies, actually," he replied, opening the back door of the Safari and inviting her to look inside.

She bent at the waist to peer into the vehicle, straightened to look at him in complete shock, and looked in again as though she didn't believe what she'd seen the first time. Then she straightened slowly and put a hand to her forehead. "I need a drink and a lemon-balm wrap," she said in a small voice. "This very instant."

ARIEL LISTENED shamelessly from the kitchen.

Duncan had chivalrously helped Phoebe Price through the kitchen and dining room to the living room, and eased her into a chair.

For someone who had the attitude of a short-haired Xena the Warrior Princess in breast armor and sword, Ariel thought, Phoebe certainly didn't have much emotional resilience.

Ariel left both babies in their carriers and proficiently held a bottle to each little mouth. While the twins ate greedily, Ariel cocked an ear toward the conversation under way in the next room.

"If you tell me those are yours," Phoebe warned Duncan, "my career as an agent is over."

Duncan replied with gentle amusement, "Shall I call your old boss at Stapleton Public Relations?"

"Deke, how could you *do* this to me?!"

There was a long pause.

"Did I…do this to *you?*" Duncan asked Phoebe.

Ariel heard the subtle sounds of fabric shifting, bodies moving. She imagined Duncan sitting on the ottoman in front of Phoebe's chair.

"What do you mean?" Phoebe asked in genuine puzzlement. "If those are your babies, of course you've done it to me. Who else could've—"

"No," he interrupted firmly. "I mean…are they your babies, too?"

Another profound silence.

Ariel closed her eyes and prayed.

DUNCAN LOOKED INTO the distressed eyes of the woman he knew so well and yet not at all, and felt great relief. He didn't think someone could fake that look of total cluelessness.

"What are you talking about?" she demanded.

He told her about the babies' abandonment at the hospital with nothing but the father's initials on the birth certificate.

"You started calling me D.K. when you first took me on," he said. "And you were at the table that night of the wrap party for *Border Incident*." He explained about waking up the following morning with only flashes of memory of the night before. "Between the painkillers and the champagne, I have no real memory of who I made love to."

She stammered as she seemed to struggle to organize her thoughts to respond. "But now everyone on the set calls you D.K. or Deke. And I wasn't the only one at that ta—" She stopped abruptly, then, bringing her fist down on the arm of the chair, said emphatically, "Drop-Drawers Delacroix!"

Duncan groaned. It was well-known that Yvette Delacroix had slept her way to leading roles, but he hated to think of her in those terms. Particularly since there was a chance that *she* was the woman from the room over the cantina.

"Is she still in the Gobi Desert?" Duncan asked.

"Far as I know," Phoebe replied, leaning back in her chair with a deep sigh, a hand to her heaving bosom. "And she was still at the table with you when I left to find a fax machine. Deke, for heaven's sake. You make me feel as though I've been beamed to Mars without my Fodor's." Then she met and held his gaze, everything about her quieting, slowing. "Do you really think there could ever have been something…between us?"

He looked right into her eyes and replied candidly but with an affectionate smile, "No." He knew she really didn't, either.

She smiled in return and sighed again. "Pity, though. Your face and talent and my savvy, we could rule Hollywood." Her expression changed suddenly from wistfulness to annoyance. "Speaking of which, did you and Steven ever get down to talking about money?"

Duncan shook his head. "No. I was never serious enough about it for that."

"He's offering…" She whispered a figure that was positively obscene.

Even Duncan was momentarily speechless. He'd

thought himself inured to astronomical figures bandied about when the principals in films were assembled, but this was cause for a reverent moment.

And the only words he could think of to say were very irreverent, so he kept them to himself.

Phoebe, however, had no such compunction. She reeled off several, her features and manner hardening again to her old standards. "It isn't every day that I have to say goodbye to my cut of that kind of money. May I ask what in heaven's name made you... Oh, no—" she seemed to have found an answer even before she'd fully formed her question "—it's that hero thing, again, isn't it? You don't think the audience will see you as anything but a villain." She leaned forward in her chair until they were almost nose to nose. "Darling, for all those millions, could you possibly think again?"

"Pheeb—"

"Deke. You're just hitting your stride as a male box-office draw. You've become a marquee actor. Your name alone brings people into the theater. And something very interesting is happening to you." She studied him a moment, her eyes growing serious, as though she was about to impart important information. "Sweetie, you're not growing into an even better, darker, more frightening villain. Something else is coming out of you. You're giving your villain depth; you're making the audience yearn for his salvation. You're turning villains into heroes, Deke. So think about taking it all the way. *Start* with a hero, and make us understand him and love him for the villain in him that he suppresses. Try it once. If you hate it, or you feel as though you've done a bad job, you never have to do it again."

She smiled and patted his cheek in a way that was almost maternal. "The audience is forgiving of the actor who gives his all. If you bomb, so what? You'll make a fortune anyway. And just do what they expect of you next time and they'll love you all over again. That's worked for Clint and Sly and Demi. Don't be afraid."

"Of course I'm afraid," he laughed, a little unnerved by her assessment of him. "I don't want to be the actor who causes Spielberg his first flop."

She leveled a severe gaze at him. "You also don't want to be the actor who beats Phoebe Price out of her percentage of that kind of money."

He leaned over to kiss her cheek again. "You don't scare me, Pheeb," he said. "I know that under that Kevlar exterior beats a marshmallow heart."

"That's a load of—"

"Ah, ah." He stopped her with a shushing finger to his lips. "Babies in the house. I promised Steven I'd call him back on the first of August. And I promise *you* I'll give it serious thought, all right?"

She looked less than satisfied, but finally she nodded. "Okay." Then she lowered her voice. "Where'd you get the nanny?" she asked, getting to her feet. "Was she free now that the Gottis are out of circulation?"

Duncan stood with her. "No mob ties. She's my sister's friend and just got out of the convent after a couple of years and needed work."

Phoebe straightened the collar of her silky white blouse and touched her throat, as though remembering Ariel's hands on her.

"Either the convent life's gotten pretty tough, honey," she said, "or your nanny wrestled for a living before she went in. Am I invited to dinner?"

Chapter Six

"You don't *look* Italian," Phoebe said, casting an assessing glance across the table at Ariel. "Of course, looks can be deceiving." She twirled spaghetti on her fork.

Ariel sprinkled more fresh grated Parmesan on what was left of her meal, while trying to fend off the prying woman's questions. "You don't have to be Italian to make great spaghetti," she said politely. She'd tried ignoring Phoebe, but the woman's interest in Ariel made that impossible. So she'd tried sidestepping her interrogation instead.

"Her name's Bonneau." Duncan passed Phoebe the tall glass that held breadsticks. "That's French." He smiled at Ariel with a questioning eyebrow raised. "Right?"

"Right," she agreed.

"And you were a nun before you came here to nanny?" As if to punctuate, Phoebe snapped a breadstick in half.

"Yes. Up until a few months ago."

"Was it a wrestling order?"

"Phoebe," Duncan said, impatience in his voice, "let up, all right. Many women are good at self-defense. You're just suspicious of her because she nailed you and you're a sore loser.''

Phoebe ignored him, and concentrated on Ariel. ''What do you call the part of the mass where the priest raises the bread and wine?''

''Pheeb!'' Duncan put his fork down. ''You're about to get yourself thrown out.''

Ariel touched his hand to stop his protest. ''It's all right. I can answer anything she asks.'' She refocused on Phoebe. ''The priest raises the bread and wine during the consecration.''

Phoebe leaned toward her. ''What's the sermon called?''

Ariel answered without hesitation, ''The homily.''

''What order did you belong to?''

''Sisters of the Holy Cross.''

''The ones with the big side-wing things like Sally Field wore as Sister Bertrille.''

Ariel shook her head. ''No. That was the Sisters of Charity, and none of the orders wear extravagant habits anymore.''

Phoebe leaned back in her chair and nodded. ''You would know all that if you simply went to Catholic school.''

Ariel shrugged. ''I did. So ask me something harder. You want to know about my postulancy? My novitiate? The Holy Father's given name? I can recite prayers from the morning office. I could describe the convent grounds, and you could go to Santa Ynez and check them out yourself.''

Phoebe brought her napkin to her lips, set it down with ceremony, and finally smiled, though there was no friendliness in the gesture.

''You *do* have answers for everything,'' she conceded. "But instead of convincing me that you're who you say you are, they've convinced me that you're not. Do you want to know why?"

Ariel turned to Duncan. "Do *you?*" she asked.

"No," he replied.

"Well, I'll tell you anyway," Phoebe insisted. Then she leaned across the table again to accuse quietly but forcefully, "You're not humble enough to have ever been a nun."

Ariel shook her head. "I'm afraid your notions of a nun's personality in the nineties are as outdated as your idea of how she dresses."

"And now the subject is closed," Duncan said firmly.

"What if she's casing you and your place for her partners in crime?" Phoebe persisted.

Ariel grinned. "You mean the other sisters in my convent?"

"All right." Phoebe raised both hands in an attitude of surrender. The right one held a fork, however, so the gesture seemed less than benign. "You say all the right things, and if you've convinced Duncan you're a nanny, you must *do* all the right things. But there's something in your energy, sweetie, that says otherwise. I feel it. You do, however, make wonderful spaghetti."

"Thank you. Butter for that breadstick?"

DUNCAN WENT TO BED shortly after midnight. He'd offered to drive Phoebe back to the Portland Airport, but she pointed to the silver Bonneville across the street.

"I got a rental so I could check out the countryside." She gave him a scolding look. "Frankly, I wasn't in a mood to notice pretty things on my way out here, but now that you've promised to at least think about Spielberg's offer, I might be able to soothe my troubled soul with the Oregon landscape.''

"You rented a *Bonneville?*" he'd teased. "Clearly mileage isn't a concern."

"Of course not." She'd reached up to kiss his cheek. Then she'd let him walk her out to her car, and had driven away while waving out the driver's window.

He'd walked back into the house, struck anew by the spicy aromas of oregano and garlic—something he seldom experienced at home in Malibu. He usually ate out, and the house—big and comfortable and cozy in its own way—smelled of the orange-and-clove potpourri the housekeeper put out for him.

Here there were dishes in the sink, coffee warming in the pot, and...the sound of a tune he couldn't put a name to sung in an unpolished but enthusiastic soprano.

He felt an odd warmth in his chest as he followed the music to his parents' bedroom. Ariel sat with the babies in the middle of the bed, singing cheerfully as she changed Gabrielle into a fresh sleeper. Michelle already wore the bright yellow-footed thing with white bears all over it.

The song was something about clouds and angels.

He watched Ariel's nimble fingers catch the active little leg and manage to snap the fabric closed around it.

He had to grant that there *was* something mysterious about her. He didn't know what it was, and for the moment he didn't really care. She was good with the twins, made great spaghetti, and was pleasant to have around. And that meant she could plug the gaps in his domestic life so that he could spend his time getting to know his daughters, and locating their mother.

Having finally dressed Gabrielle, Ariel leaned over both babies and nuzzled first one face, then the other, still singing her nonsense song. The twins responded with happy noises, little legs kicking.

"Even if you did belong to a wrestling order," he teased, walking into the room, "I appreciate the good job you're doing."

Ariel turned to him, shaking her head with a frown. "Can you imagine? I hope she's a better agent than she is a judge of human nature."

He lifted Gabrielle into his arms, settled her on his left side, then held his right arm so that Ariel could put Michelle in it.

"She is. I don't know what got into her, but I apologize."

"It was probably your turning down the Steven Spielberg thing. She wanted to take exception to every other decision you've made, including having babies and hiring a nanny."

"I'm sure you're right." He headed for the door, then asked over his shoulder, "Could you grab the blanket on the shelf in the closet? I'll lay the girls on the living room floor for a while so we can get better acquainted. You've put in a long day today. I didn't really expect you to cook, you know."

She opened the closet and reached up to the shelf, but it was an inch or so higher than the reach of her fingertips.

"Oh, I don't mind. I love to cook as long as you don't expect gourmet meals." She looked around, probably for something to stand on, but there was nothing more substantial in the room than wicker.

He came up behind her, about to tell her that if she held one of the babies, he would get the blanket. Suddenly she jumped up, caught the top of the doorframe in one hand and, while suspended, reached in for the blanket and pulled. It dropped into her arms as she landed on her feet.

Interesting, he thought. A wrestling, *acrobatic* order.

She spread the blanket for him and helped him place the babies on it.

"I put your things in the room across from mine," he told her, sitting on an edge of the blanket. "The room Dillon, Harper and Darian tried to vacate for you yesterday. But you don't have to stay out of the way or anything. You're welcome to watch television or put in a video if you want to." He grinned. "As long as it isn't one of mine. I'll start analyzing my performance and I'm supposed to be on vacation."

"I think I would like to go upstairs," she said. "Put my things away, read for a while. Do you mind if I take a cup of tea with me?"

"Not at all. Just treat the house as though it were yours."

"Thank you." She turned at the dining room doorway. "Good night."

He waved her on. "Sleep well."

The babies were wide awake for several hours. If he'd fallen in love with them at first sight, he was now completely besotted. They smiled for him and reacted to his efforts to entertain them as though he were the cleverest, most brilliant being on the face of the earth. When he held a finger out to them, Michelle grabbed it and held on for several seconds. Gabrielle bit it firmly with her gums.

It was after ten when they finally went to sleep. He gathered in the edges of the blanket, wrapped it around both of them, and carried them up to the portable crib in his room.

He noticed that the door was closed to Ariel's room, and that there was no light showing underneath.

He put the babies down, loving the way they snuggled into each other without waking.

Taking a quick shower with the bathroom door open so that he could be alert to sounds from the babies, he toweled off, pulled on dark-blue silk pajama bottoms, and climbed into bed with the local weekly paper he'd picked up at the market. He dozed off in the middle of an article on beach erosion.

He woke up to the sound of a high, shrill scream.

For an instant, he thought one of the babies had awakened. Darrick and Dillon had warned him that though the twins had been sleeping through the night more often, they still awakened once in a while with loud demands for formula or attention.

He was up like a shot, but soon realized the sound wasn't from the crib.

Again he heard the scream, this time followed by running footsteps in the hall. It was Ariel!

He ran to the bedroom door and yanked it open.

"No!" Ariel's voice cried. He watched her round the end of the corridor, then heard her run down the stairs. "No, please! He'll fall!"

Duncan flipped lights on as he ran after her and caught up with her in the living room, where she was running first one way and then the other as though trapped or confused.

"Ariel?" he said quietly as she approached her. "What is it?"

She wore a black silk nightshirt, and her throat and face rose out of it as though cut from paper—white and bloodless. Her eyes were enormous and unfocused, as though she saw something that wasn't in the room.

He was now close enough to touch her and did so carefully, a hand to her arm to steady her. "Ariel? Are you awake?"

She looked at him, but he didn't see recognition in her eyes. He guessed that she was still snared by the fringes of a nightmare.

She turned the arm he held to catch his forearm in her hand.

"Help me!" she said urgently. "He's falling."

He felt the tremor in her arm, saw it in her bottom lip and her chin. He pulled her into his free arm because she still had a death grip on his other.

"Who's falling?" he asked.

She shook her head, and her eyes widened even further, horror in them. She screamed again as though seeing what she so seemed to fear.

Duncan wrapped his arms around her, pressing her close to him in the hope that human contact would comfort her, awaken her.

As she sobbed against his shoulder, he rocked her gently from side to side, told her it was all right, that she was all right, that it was just a dream.

Then, as though someone had flipped a switch, she stiffened in his arms and drew back. She looked around her, then up at him. But when he thought she would step back, mortified to find herself in his arms, she moved toward him instead, her face crumpling.

She wept quietly, this time obviously completely aware of what she was doing.

He held her, patting her back, repeating words of reassurance.

"I'm sorry," she sniffed, still holding on to him as though he were the mast of a floundering boat. He had a swift mental image of what Darrick and Dillon had told him about the ship that had broken up offshore in the last century with the dancers aboard.

But this was no memory or ghost with her arms around him, holding on for dear life. The woman and her desperation were very real.

"There's nothing to apologize for," he said, leaning his cheek against her hair. "I used to have bad dreams about a giant lizard that ate my stuff."

She stopped crying after a moment, sniffed and looked up at him, clearly puzzled. "What stuff?"

"Whatever I needed," he replied, arms still around her. "My homework, my paper-route money, the transcripts of my grades, my director."

She smiled thinly at that and swiped at her eyes with one hand. "You're making this up to make me feel better," she accused in a raspy voice.

He ran a hand gently up and down her spine. "Is it working?"

She drew a deep breath and nodded. "Yeah. Thanks."

And that was the moment when he became aware that the shirt only skimmed the middle of her thighs and that she was probably naked under it. That he wore no shirt, and that one of her hands was splayed against the middle of his back just above his first lumbar vertebra. That he could feel the softness of a breast against his rib cage through the silk of her shirt. That she had a knee between his.

And that she was sharply aware of all these things, too.

ARIEL'S EVERY INSTINCT told her this was not the moment. Back away. *Go* away!

But Duncan McKeon had his arms wrapped around her, had followed her as she ran in panic, had drawn her into his arms and comforted her.

She couldn't run. She could only look up into his eyes and see everything life had so far refused her. Her life had always been about self-denial—and she was tired of it.

She felt the warm, hard muscle of his back under her hand, the big, inviting wall of his chest against her breast, the strong line of his shoulder on a level with her lips.

She turned her head very deliberately and planted a kiss there. It smelled of powdered babies and a musky cologne.

She felt the ripple of reaction in him, and looked up just as his head came down. She felt like a volcano, like the lightning in a storm, like the blue heart of a flame.

His mouth opened on hers with the same power, but his approach changed in an instant to one of tenderness rather than passion. And it completely disarmed her.

His hand came to her face, cushioning her cheek as he kissed her with all the gentle interest of a kind man exploring an embrace with an ex-nun.

She responded as gently and was rewarded with

sensation that seemed intensified by the delicacy with which it was approached.

She felt the shape of his lips against hers, the light scrape of his beard, the mild roughness of his chest hair against the inside of her arm, the definition of his every fingerprint where his hands touched her shoulder and her back.

Then, as though he'd frightened her—or himself— he took her firmly by the shoulders and stood her away from him. He studied her in what appeared to be astonishment.

"I'm sorry," he said after a moment.

She blinked at him. "Whatever for?"

He seemed to struggle over a reply. "I was just trying to… No, I didn't mean to…that is…"

She rolled her eyes and smiled. "I know. You can't stop thinking of me as a nun. But I'm not anymore, remember?"

He smiled with her for a moment, then he sobered suddenly and shook his head. "No," he said, and before he even explained precisely what that negative meant, she heard the finality in it. "I'm sorry because…I shouldn't have. I'm trying to find the twins' mother, and…she has to be my…priority."

Well. That was unexpected. Maybe she should have seen it coming, but she hadn't. "I see." This had been all her fault after all. She made herself smile at him. "Well, I'm so sorry I woke you. I…good night."

She turned and ran for the stairs, wishing she could be scooped up by some powerful hand and carried to Nova Scotia where she could hit Dori with a blunt object.

Duncan watched her hurry for the stairs, the backs of her bare, slender legs under the short hem of her nightshirt catching and holding his gaze. He fought competing feelings of guilt and lust.

She's an ex-nun, for God's sake, he thought, smiling at the irony of the expression. A friend of his sister. A lonely young woman trying to rebuild her life. She was understandably vulnerable to gestures of kindness and comfort.

He'd just been reacting like a big brother, he told himself as he went back through the house, turning off lights. When she'd been running around like a wild woman, he'd followed to protect her, unsure of the nature of the threat. Then, when he'd realized she'd had a nightmare, he'd wanted to comfort her.

That had been the mistake. She'd felt soft and small in his arms, and the feel of her had ignited mutual interest and attraction.

And he'd reacted like the villain of the piece, taking advantage of her vulnerability, of her understandable confusion in mistaking her own need for comfort for a need for…sex.

Because that was what he'd wanted all right.

Damn. He turned off the light in the kitchen and climbed the stairs into the dimly lit hallway. Her door was closed. All was quiet.

He checked the babies and found them still sleeping soundly. Then he slipped back into bed, telling himself there'd been no serious harm done.

Tomorrow they would establish a business-like routine that he would hold to until Dori came home—or until he found the mother of his babies.

Then his life would be simplified. They would be a family. Well, maybe she wouldn't want to be a family, but at least he would know who she was.

He punched his pillow and buried his face in it,

trying to erase the image behind his eyes of slender, muscular thighs and calves running away from him.

Abruptly he raised his head in the darkness and wondered, *What is an ex-nun doing in black silk anyway?*

ARIEL ACCEPTED that night as a step backward. She knew that forward progress would be made only if she ignored it entirely and went along with the friendly but more formal working atmosphere Duncan put in place the following morning.

He bade her a pleasant good-morning, then each of them fed a twin, ate breakfast, changed a twin.

He left her to dress them, saying he was going to buy rosebushes for the side of the house. "After lunch," he said, "you can have a couple of hours off to do whatever you want to do."

"I can take the twins to town while you put the roses in." She looked into his face with a carefully neutral expression. Her eyes wanted to wander over his great shoulders in the simple cotton T-shirt, his long, lean legs in old denim. "I'd like to get some beads."

"Rosary beads?"

She was beginning to get impatient with his constant reference to the convent. But she replied patiently, "No. Beads for the skirt Harper made for Olivia's wedding dress."

He shook his head in amusement. "You believe in that stuff?"

She took exception to the word "stuff." "You mean love that transcends death? Of course I do. That's what Christianity is all about."

"All right, that's true. But why would Olivia bring

half a wedding dress to this house? She never knew and couldn't possibly love *us*."

"Why not? Lovers love other lovers because they understand them."

That was getting entirely too close to the few minutes last night they'd carefully skated around all morning. He decided to back out of the conversation.

"Anything you need from the nursery?" he asked as he headed for the front door.

She smiled. "No, thanks. But don't forget the window boxes Dori wanted."

"That's right." He pulled the door open, remembering the conversation they'd had when he'd picked her up at the airport. "With pink nasturtiums. I'll get those after the roses are in. I'll be back in an hour."

Duncan bought light-pink sweet-sixteen roses, red saturnia and white snowbirds. He planned to put a fragrant saturnia right under his parents' bedroom window.

The clerk helped him carry his purchases out to the car, and Duncan was almost surprised to find it surrounded by fans, apparently waiting for a glimpse of him.

He waved and smiled, realizing that for the first time in many years, he'd gone out without thinking about his fame and what it would mean to his ability to shop in peace.

That wouldn't have alarmed him except that it meant he'd had something more pressing on his mind: Ariel.

He put her resolutely out of his thoughts, checked his watch, and, seeing that he wasn't due home for another twenty minutes, went to the Buckley Arms' coffee bar. Dillon had told him that they made great espresso.

Finding the place empty, he went inside, looking forward to a quiet few minutes and a quick jolt of caffeine.

The young man behind the counter, however, was chatty.

"Devlin Cross—" the boy started listing Duncan's roles "—Peter Jacobi, Iago, the Sheriff of Nottingham, Count Dracula." The boy leaned his elbows on the counter, as Duncan sprinkled chocolate powder onto his steamed milk. "What's it like to be able to be bad with all those gorgeous babes?"

Duncan grinned. "It's great," he replied, going to a small table where a spindly little chair looked as if it might not hold him. The boy followed, smiling with satisfaction over his reply.

Duncan added with a seriousness he realized he might not have had before he discovered he had two daughters, "But that's because none of it's real. And when you see the bad end Devlin and the others come to, it makes you think about how much closer you can get to a woman when you're good to her."

"Yeah, I know," the boy admitted grudgingly. "I just thought it might be cool to be in a situation where you don't have to worry about consequences."

"No such thing," Duncan said. "Good fiction has consequences, too."

The boy nodded and extended a hand. "Jeremy Boswell."

Duncan took it. "Duncan McKeon. I'm staying in the Buckley house."

"I know. My mom helped your brother and his lady with their research about the family."

"Right. I saw the pictures."

"Your brother bought my mom's desk. It used to belong to Alice Buckley. That's where she found the pictures."

"I heard about that."

"You seen the ghost?"

"Not a sign."

"You think she's there?"

"No."

The boy looked surprised. "Why not?"

"Because…I only believe what I know to be true."

Jeremy's puzzlement deepened. "But you make movies."

Duncan had to admit that the boy had him there. It was true that that position made no sense in view of what he did for a living.

Did that mean he had to rethink Olivia?

He decided that what it *did* mean was that he had to get a lid for his espresso, and look for peace and quiet elsewhere.

He did not find that peace and quiet at home. For reasons neither he nor Ariel could explain, the twins were fussy. They were happy enough when held, but putting either of them down resulted in whines that quickly turned to screeches.

Ariel produced an ear thermometer that Harper had left for her, but the babies' temperatures weren't elevated. And they were fed, dry, burped and free of rashes or any apparent injury.

Then an upsetting thought occurred to Duncan. "You think they miss Dillon?" he asked Ariel. "Or Darrick? Or Skye and Harper?"

Ariel shook her head, bouncing Michelle while pulling things one-handed out of the cupboard. "I think they got used to a lot of company, a lot of activity, and things are quiet again. Or maybe they're just having a down day. You know. A little case of the blues.''

"The blues? At nine weeks old?"

"Why not? Feelings are feelings, whether you're nine weeks old or ninety years. So we'll just be cheerful, fill the house with music and homey aromas, and they'll feel reassured.''

He looked doubtful as he patted Gabrielle's back. She'd quieted for a few minutes, but the line of her lip was uncertain, as though she might burst into tears at any moment.

"What are you making?'' he asked Ariel, studying the can of cling peaches, the jar of apricot jam, and the collection of spices.

She reached into the refrigerator and pulled a foam tray out of the meat-keeper. "Pork chops,'' she said, handing them to him. "Carrots, cauliflower, or corn? Or any combination of the above?''

"How about carrots and cauliflower.''

"Okay. And do you like your brownies chocolate or blonde?''

"Blonde?''

She tossed him a bag of carrots, then pulled a head of cauliflower out of the vegetable crisper. She kicked the refrigerator door closed. "You know—brownies made with brown sugar and butter instead of chocolate.''

He frowned. "Never heard of them.''

"Well,'' she said with an exaggerated sweep of the cauliflower. "There's been a terrible gap in your culinary education. After dinner, you're going to meet a delicious blonde.''

"Really.'' Something curious was happening here.

There was a subtle change in Ariel. The quiet young woman who'd arrived two days ago, looking a little wary and very plain, seemed to have gained confidence and a curious glow he couldn't explain.

She wore no makeup that he could see, and there might be a little more...fluff to her hair. But she seemed quite pretty, more pink-cheeked and bright-eyed than the shy young woman he'd picked up at the airport.

He couldn't account for that. Unless it was that things were going reasonably well. She did a great job with the babies, and must be feeling appreciated for her cooking and her good humor. Maybe that was all it took to brighten an outlook and, therefore, a face.

"Really," she said. "Shall I sing, or do we have a disc player, or something?"

He shook his head. "No, a stereo is something we're lacking. But I could put a music channel on the television. MTV or the Country Music Channel?"

"I guess country would be more soothing to the babies."

He laughed and went to turn it on. "You're sure that's the right thing?" he asked as Reba McIntyre bemoaned a wayward lover. "Isn't country music all about love and loss and homes breaking up?"

She pulled two squares of fabric out of a bottom drawer and handed him one. "Yes, but fortunately the girls can't understand the words, and the music's mellow. These are those front packs the neighbor lady made for the babies. At least they'll leave our hands free to work."

She handed him Michelle while she pulled hers on then tied it at the back of her waist. Then she reclaimed the twin and slipped her into it. Michelle protested at first, apparently on principle, then quieted again.

Ariel helped him with his, then smiled with satisfaction as both babies sat quietly in their packs.

Gabrielle's legs worked against Duncan's stomach, as though she expected action of some kind.

"It's clear I'm not going to get the roses in today," he said, patting the baby's back. "But maybe I can get the window boxes painted so we can put yours up tomorrow. Sorry about your trip to town for beads."

She shrugged. "I can get them just as well tomorrow."

"Good."

A couple of hours later Duncan sat down to pork chops topped with peaches in apricot glaze and thought it was one of the most delicious meals he'd ever had. The vegetables were seasoned to perfection, and his simple baked potato was perfectly done and drenched in butter.

"It's that phony butter," she told him as she passed it to him across the kitchen table. "But it's good, isn't it?"

And it was—in more ways than one.

He hated to admit it even to himself, but although the brownies made with brown sugar were absolutely delicious, he found himself falling in love that night, not with a blonde—but with a brunette.

Chapter Seven

Ariel went up into the attic the following morning to study Olivia's bodice and to plan her beads purchase. The twins were their cheerful, smiley selves today and she took them up with her, Michelle in the pack, Gabrielle in her arms.

The attic was bathed in light, and Ariel placed both babies on the bed in the sunbeam from the window. She leaned over them and nuzzled first one, then the other, her heart swelling with love. Her daughters, at last.

"Oh, babies," she crooned, arms wrapped around both of them. "Mama's here. You don't have to worry about who you belong to anymore. I'm here." Tears brimmed in her eyes. She wept for the terrible lonely months, for the hiding, for the abiding pain of loving a man, for bringing two beautiful babies into the world and having to walk away from all of them for their own protection.

"I've missed you so much. But everything's going to be all right now. All we have to do is explain to your father what happened—when the time is right."

Michelle rubbed her eyes. Gabrielle yawned widely.

Ariel laughed through her tears. "I know. Excuses

are boring, but I have a good one. It's just a lot to go into right now. And just between you and me, I think Olivia came to help us.''

Ariel went to put her hand to the dress. ''She knew I'd come here to find you and your dad—to reclaim you. Well, here I am, and I'm going to finally settle up. I'm going to end the spectre of the threat to my family, finish the dress, and settle my father's future, then my own—for better or worse.''

And then, because she'd taken the dress as a sign the first moment she'd seen it, she wrapped her arms around it as though it contained a loved one who could offer comfort. She'd been separated from her babies so much longer than she'd planned. And from Duncan.

She'd been surprised to discover when she arrived here several days ago that being with him and being unable to tell him who she was was almost more painful than being apart from him.

It had been easy to deceive Phoebe Price, she thought wryly, but it had hurt to lie to Skye and Harper. Dori had explained that both were forceful and determined, and that sharing the truth with them might mean they would try to take steps to solve her problems. Or what was worse—they would tell their husbands, who would come to the defense of their brother and his babies, and destroy the careful plans she'd spent the last year putting in place.

That was the same reason she had to keep her identity secret from Duncan. His instinctive reaction—presuming he would even care about her life after learning the truth—would be to take care of the problem for her. And she couldn't allow him to do that. The safety of everyone she loved was at stake.

Ariel lifted her head and stepped back from the

wedding dress, sniffing and pulling herself together. "When I first arrived, babies, I wasn't sure what I could hope for. I thought I might just have to watch for the right moment and take you away. But the dress was a message to me; I know that. I've fought for the kind of family I wanted my whole life, and it isn't over yet. I have to fight for your dad, too." She drew a deep breath and rubbed her eyes with the back of her hand. "We're going to ask Olivia to hold the good thought for us." Then she was able to smile as a warming thought occurred to her. "I wonder if she knows your Grandma Godinez and your Uncle Donovan. Maybe she could say hello for us."

DUNCAN LOOKED UP from smoothing planting soil into the hole in which he'd placed a saturnia rosebush, and saw Ariel coming toward him, pushing the twins in their carriage. She wore her baggy jeans and a pink T-shirt, and her brow was furrowed as though she bore some troublesome burden.

She looked up at him just before she reached him, and he noticed that her cheeks were pale, her nose red, and her eyes soupy as though she'd been ill—or crying.

"Hi," she said, her voice sounding raspy and a little thin as she parked the carriage nearby. "They'll be comfortable in here while I go to town. And you'll be able to keep working. Is that okay?"

He rose instinctively, pulled off a gardening glove and, when she turned to him, reached an arm out for her.

"Something wrong?" he asked gently.

She leaned into him gratefully, hiding her face

against his chest. He thought he felt a sob ripple through her.

He tossed both gloves onto the grass and wrapped his arms around her. This wasn't healthy, he knew. She was the nanny, he was the employer. He was a man looking for the mother of his children; she was an ex-nun come to help him while he searched.

But safe or not, she seemed to need him. And he'd been an older brother too long to resist a protective impulse. He ignored the fact that he felt something other than brotherly affection, preferring not to think about how convoluted his life was becoming.

"Nothing's wrong," she finally replied, her voice muffled against the front of his shirt. "It's just not right, exactly."

"What isn't right?"

"Everything."

He rubbed her back and laughed softly. "Well, that makes it pretty hard for me to fix. Do you mean just 'everything' personal, or things cosmic also?"

That had the desired result. She drew a step back from him and gave him that reluctant smile he so often saw in her. She took a tissue out of her jeans pocket and dabbed at her nose.

"What makes you think *you* have to fix it?" she asked. "Dori says you're always slaying dragons for her, but you're not *my* big brother."

The look in her eye said that she was making that distinction very deliberately. He dropped his arms from her, struggling to put a distance between them.

"It's a custodial world. We help each other."

She seemed to be assessing him. He got the unsettling feeling that she could read his innermost thoughts. Possibly even the label on his underwear.

"I can't understand," she said, a tone of real puzzlement in her voice, "how you ever got this perception of yourself as a villain. You're so...good."

That was definitely something he was not going to go into on a sunny July morning with his twins sleeping peacefully, the scent of roses in the air, and Ariel clearly beset by her own problems.

"It's a long story," he said, reaching to the grass to snatch up his gloves. Then he grinned. "Maybe one day when we know each other better..."

She nodded, smiling privately. "Fair enough." She pointed in the direction of town. "Is there anything you need while I'm looking for beads?"

"Nothing."

"What if I bring back soft tacos and nachos?"

"I would be eternally grateful. We can eat in the backyard under the ash tree."

WANDERING DOWNTOWN Dancer's Beach, purse slung over her shoulder and hands in the pockets of her jeans, Ariel Bonneau morphed back into Julietta Godinez: nanny, translator, and former cat burglar.

She drew the comfortably warm waterfront air into her lungs as she walked and marveled that she was here in this little slice of coastal Americana. For the last year she'd felt as though she'd been balanced on her back on the tip of a sword suspended over a snake pit.

She shook that feeling off as she breathed deeply of Dancer's Beach. She smiled as she thought of that visit she'd had at age twelve from her mother. She'd promised that everything would be fine and that she'd find lasting happiness. She just hadn't mentioned how awful it would be in between.

Not that her life had been terrible. The off-season with her father and younger brothers on the little ranch outside of El Paso had been nice. She and Mike and Eddie had gone to school, hung out with friends, done all the things other families did—except have a mother. And a father with a nine-to-five job.

But the moment early summer came and wealthy tourists were on the move to posh resorts and resplendent hotels across the country, her father would gather up his children, his brother-in-law, his nephew, and two of his childhood friends, and they became a gang of slick jewel thieves, so swift and efficient that they'd evaded the police for years.

Her father had taken great pride in the success of their family venture and the relief it brought to the Hidalgo region of Mexico where he'd grown up. After fencing the jewels, he kept enough to keep the family through the winter, then sent everything else back to Mexico with Baldo, Julie's uncle, and Sal, her cousin.

Then Baldo had died and one of her father's friends, Emilion Suarez, had taken over the planning aspect Baldo had always handled.

When Julie had been young, she'd thought the work heroic. But as she grew older and developed a social conscience—one more traditional than her father's—she began to change her opinion of "the business."

There was no doubt that the money derived from the things her father stole accomplished great things for his old friends and neighbors. But he'd *stolen* it, and she could no longer reconcile the result with how it was achieved.

And as her love for her family grew, she found herself in constant terror that one of them would fall, or be shot, or simply be arrested and finally jailed.

She'd pleaded with her father many times to stop, but he insisted that the work was important.

The day she learned she'd earned a scholarship to study languages at UCLA, she formally resigned from the "Cat Pack," as the press had come to call them.

Her father had pleaded, shouted, berated, but she'd held firm.

After that, visits home just resulted in arguments, so she'd stayed away, praying for her family's safety and their eventual decision to pursue another line of work.

Shortly after she left the gang, her father's friends Suarez and Cisco Martin also left—over a dispute about the money. They thought that it was time the gang kept more of it. Her father had disagreed.

Early last year, a guard had been shot in the robbery of a hotel in New York City. The headlines had speculated on whether Diego Godinez and his gang had been responsible.

Several years after she'd graduated from college, her father had visited her in Los Angeles. She'd been thrilled, hopeful that he would tell her the Godinez family business was going legitimate.

Instead he had tried to solicit her help in the theft of a set of diamond-and-emerald necklace and earrings from a home on the Vieux Carré in New Orleans. Entry through an oculus window would minimize danger and cut the time spent inside in half. "Cisco could have gotten in," he'd said, "but he abandoned me, too."

Disappointed and angry, she'd refused to help and had even threatened to turn him into the police.

"Miguel and Eduardo should be learning to keep their feet on the ground, not to run around rooftops, supporting your warped notion of community service! You're playing a dangerous game, Papa. Now guards are getting shot.''

He'd drawn himself up in an imperious huff, but his eyes betrayed genuine hurt. "We've drifted farther apart than I'd imagined, *hija,* if you think me guilty of such a thing.''

He'd stalked away, also disappointed and angry.

The next night she'd been awakened by a telephone call from Cisco, telling her that her father had been set up, and that the police had been waiting in New Orleans.

"Sal got everyone away," he said, "but your father fell and broke his arm. He's all right, *chica,* but *you* are in danger. The police are looking for you to make you tell them where your father is.''

She surfaced from the shock of the news to challenge the one-time family friend.

"Why are you calling me, Cisco? You left my father to work with Suarez.''

"I did," he admitted. "I wanted more money. But I did not want to hurt anyone. Suarez, however, has no such concerns! He pulled the job where the guard was shot—not your father. And I can get the film to prove it, but it will take some time.

"Since that job, I've been reporting Suarez's plans to Diego so that he could do the job first. But Suarez must have found out and knew when he told me about the New Orleans job that I would tell your father. He set us up, *chica.* You must hide until I can get this tape to you.''

"The police wouldn't hurt me, Cisco. This isn't Mexico.''

"Listen to me! Suarez wants you, too. You must hide—and you must do it *now!*"

"What does Suarez want with me?"

"If he had you, he could force your father to come out of hiding and accomplish what the betrayal in New Orleans failed to do. Please, Julietta—"

Then there'd been a shout, the sound of breaking glass—and the call was terminated.

Julie had run to Dori, who'd hidden her in her apartment for several days. Dori had come home excitedly one day to tell her that her brother was in the cast of a film looking for a translator to work with them in Mexico. They needed someone to deal with extras.

Dori had said her brother had laughed about the fact that a southern California crew had no one in their number who spoke Spanish.

"I didn't say anything about you," Dori assured her, "but I happen to know who to call. You can just say that word got around. It always does when they're putting together a crew."

That had seemed like a heaven-sent solution, because it would take Julie beyond the reach of the police. And Suarez scorned the pervasive poverty of his homeland; he never returned.

Julie had called the number Dori provided, not mentioning her connection to Dori. Two days later she was working on a film in Mexico.

And then she'd met Duncan McKeon and had fallen instantly in love, giving her already upside-down life a sideways spin.

Little had she known then that it would take Cisco a year to find and copy the incriminating film—and that she would be living by her wits all that time.

Memories of the past year always exhausted her, but

firmed her determination to see this through. Julie reached the craft shop and paused before going inside. She held her family's faces in mind for a moment, then pushed open the door and went inside, slipping once again into the persona of Ariel Bonneau.

THE FEELING OF being watched developed slowly. She didn't sense it at all when she went into the fabric store that doubled as a craft shop. And she was too thrilled when she found an entire department devoted to beads to think about anything else but matching the design on the bodice of Olivia's dress with the crystal bugle beads and pearls in the scores of tiny bins.

She spent most of an hour selecting and counting and going over the pattern she'd created on the back of a grocery bag. She bought chalk to trace the pattern onto the fabric, thread to do the beading and a packet of needles.

The feeling began as she dawdled and window-shopped on her way back to the car. A little prickle of awareness ran along the back of her neck and into her scalp as she passed the edge of a park that took up two blocks.

The other end of the park was filled with children on playground equipment, some adults playing badminton, and other less industrious visitors picnicking or lying on blankets in the sun.

Dogs barked and birds sang, but it was what she couldn't see and hear that alarmed her. Or who.

Had the police finally found her? Or Suarez?

Or was it Cisco? He had a way of turning up when she was sure no one would be able to find her. But in the past he had always called.

The last time he'd called, he'd told her Suarez was

laying low in the Caymans after pulling a job on the Riviera. That was the only reason she'd felt safe in coming to Duncan and the twins. Suarez wouldn't leave his hiding place until the furor had blown over—and that could take weeks.

He'd also told her that he'd wrested the film from Suarez's hiding place and was now having it copied—no small feat while remaining underground so that Suarez wouldn't find *him*.

His message that he now *had* the copy meant she could finally put her own life back together.

She stopped in the middle of the sidewalk and looked carefully all around her. She saw nothing suspicious. No one mysterious. Was she imagining the whole thing? she wondered. After more than a year on the run, she was sometimes startled by her own reflection.

She picked up her pace and hurried to the car, thoughts of Duncan and the babies drawing her home. She'd spent so long away from them for their own protection. Now she found herself longing for them when they were apart even for a short time.

She picked up the promised soft tacos and nachos, and headed home.

Duncan was friendly and full of witty conversation, but she felt the distance he kept between them as though it were a giant chasm—and there was no bridge, not even a rope one.

She knew what he was doing. He was attracted to her, possibly even had some memory of her he couldn't understand, but he was intent on finding the twins' mother in the hope of assembling a family.

She wanted to tell him the truth, but she couldn't do that until she had the issues of Suarez and her father resolved. She had to be free to do whatever Duncan wanted to do to save the relationship.

So she tried hard to keep her place. But her body, her soul, remembered him and that night above the cantina. She wanted that for them for the rest of their lives—the love, the passion, the tenderness, the cherishing.

It was hard to keep what she felt for him out of her eyes. She knew it was there when she looked at him because it filled her being, simmering in her with all it could mean for their lives together.

She assured herself that he had to care, too. A man couldn't show a woman the degree of caring he'd shown that night, then cast her aside over actions for which she'd had no real choice.

Still, her decision to keep her distance from him and leave her babies in the care of his brothers had turned his entire family upside down, caused his brothers pain, endangered his sister, tortured everyone. That would be hard to forgive.

After lunch Duncan went back to the roses. Ariel fed the now wide-awake babies, changed them, and played with them on a blanket on the sofa, marveling at the little miracles she'd created.

She knew in her heart—as Gabrielle held her index finger with surprising strength—that she'd never be able to leave them again. And that was bound to mean war with Duncan if he couldn't understand and accept what she'd done.

LIFE WENT ON for the next week in a pleasant and torturous sort of limbo. Ariel cooked. Duncan bought and put in an arbor in the backyard. And the babies grew more and more responsive and captivating.

Ariel could sit with them for hours and be delighted by their bright eyes noticing toys, reaching for them in apparent fascination.

Duncan was entranced by the infants, also, and seemed to enjoy the sight of her holding them. She spent some time every afternoon in the sunny backyard with the babies in her lap, listening to music and enjoying the serenity of the idyllic surroundings.

Duncan liked to play with them in the hammock, the babies lying on his chest, strengthening their neck muscles as they craned their little heads up, following every sound.

Then, on Tuesday morning Phoebe called.

Duncan took the call in the kitchen, Michelle riding his arm. Ariel mixed pancake batter at the counter, while Gabrielle watched from her infant seat.

Strain became audible in his voice. "How long's she going to be there?" he asked. He listened a moment, then added tersely, "No, I appreciate your letting me know, Pheeb. Thanks." Another hesitation, then a deep spattering of laughter. "Thank you, I'll bear that in mind. Though why would you want to marry me? You'd lose your ten percent."

Another pause, then he said mildly, "Oh, Phoebe, you're so bad. No, I haven't thought about it yet. I promised I'd call on the first—and I will. So, until then, drop it, okay? Great. Thanks for the tip. Bye."

He opened the cupboard, caught two glasses in his fingers and brought them down to the counter.

"That was Phoebe," he said. "Jeanine Curry is in Ashland for a couple of days."

Jeanine, Ariel knew, was the camerawoman who'd been at Duncan's table that night. Guilt struck a match inside her; she could guess what was coming.

"They're filming a movie in Ashland?" she asked for something to say to hide her distress.

"No." He got the pitcher of orange juice out of the refrigerator and filled the two glasses. "Seems her younger sister is in one of the Shakespearean plays, and she promised to film it for some promotional thing the theater is doing."

"And you're going to talk to her."

"Yes. Will you be all right alone with the twins if I'm gone for a night or two?"

She could come clean and take her chances rather than let him make an unnecessary trip. She even opened her mouth to make the effort, but the words wouldn't come. What if she did, and he insisted on calling the police, or confronting Suarez or getting in touch with her father?

Until she had everything in place, she couldn't risk the possibility that he would call danger upon himself and the twins.

An unnecessary trip and a possibly embarrassing conversation with the camerawoman were a safer bet. So she kept the truth to herself.

"We'll be fine," she said, flipping a pancake. "When are you leaving?"

He carried first one glass of juice, then the other, to the table. "I thought I'd go right after breakfast. I can be there by early afternoon and if I can get some private time with her over dinner or drinks, I can be back in the morning."

"Okay."

She wasn't sure why she asked the next question. When she thought about it later, she considered it a little cruel. But she wondered what was on his mind, and what alternatives he was prepared for.

"What...if she is the one?" she asked, adding the pancake to a plate warming in the oven. "Will you bring her back?"

He sat at the table and held Michelle up in front of him, as though trying to judge by her features whether she resembled the camerawoman. "If she's willing. Though I suppose it's possible she might not be if she left the babies at the hospital."

"Why do you think she did that?"

He shook his head pensively. "I'm not sure. But I don't think it could have been a careless gesture. She's very career-minded, but she's warm and funny and not the kind of woman to deliberately hurt someone."

Ariel felt herself tense. So, he *had* tried to understand why the babies were abandoned in the hospital.

"She might have been frightened by the responsibility," he said, making faces at the smiling baby. "Or afraid I wouldn't care or want to help."

"She might be really thrilled to know how much you love the twins. She might want to take up with the three of you after all."

She waited for his response to that. It didn't come. He simply pulled Michelle to his shoulder and kissed her cheek.

She wondered what his silence meant. That he might understand what had motivated the babies' mother, but wasn't willing to marry her? But he'd once said that he wanted to bring all of them together as a family. Maybe his silence meant that something else had since changed his mind. Or someone.

She prayed that someone else was her.

FINDING JEANINE was amazingly simple. She answered the door of her sister's apartment in jeans and a sweatshirt bearing the face of Edgar Allen Poe. Her dark hair was atumble about a very pretty, dark-eyed face, and she had a half-eaten apple in one hand.

Duncan's attention riveted on her hair, remembering with debilitating clarity how his mystery-lover's hair had felt skimming along his flesh in the wake of her kisses.

Her eyes widened when she saw him, and she threw her arms around him with genuine delight. "Deke!" she screamed. "What are you doing here?" She looked behind him. "I can't believe there isn't a mob following you. It would have done so much more for my celebrity appeal if someone had actually seen Duncan McKeon coming up to visit me!"

He kissed her cheek. "Hi, Jeanine. Can I come in for a few minutes? I promise not to keep you."

"Of course." She stepped aside to let him in. The apartment was small and decorated with modern, brightly colored furnishings. A man about his own age in a chambray shirt and khaki shorts tried to turn a glower into a polite smile as he drew himself reluctantly out of the corner of a very uncomfortable-looking dark-blue sofa.

"My sister's at rehearsal," she said, leading Duncan toward the sofa. "She's going to hate having missed you. Deke, this is Tom Royce, my fiancé. I got a couple of days off and he came to join me." She frowned suddenly. "How'd you know where to find me, anyway?"

He shook hands with the disgruntled-looking man, guessing his unannounced arrival had interrupted something, and realizing also that if Jeanine *was* the woman from that night in Mexico, she'd apparently gotten over him. Very quickly.

"Phoebe told me," he answered. "Thank you," he added, as she gestured him to sit.

He did so, thinking that the sofa had all the comfort of a padded church pew. The back was at a complete right angle to the seat and forced him to sit up straight.

"What did you want to talk about?" she asked, her eyes bright with interest. "Don't tell me you've finally noticed my brilliant close-ups and you want me for your Spielberg film."

He looked at her in surprise. "How'd you know about that?"

She shrugged. "Everyone knows. It might be Phoebe. She's always boasting about your next project."

And the more she talked it up, he guessed, the more pressure would be put on him to do the film. Gossip in Hollywood often became fact, whether it started that way or not.

He shook his head. "Sorry, that's not it. But if I do agree to do it, I'll ask for you."

"All *right*. So, what's up?"

Duncan turned apologetically to Jeanine's fiancé. "May I speak to Jeanine privately, please?"

The man's manner shifted from disgruntled to indignant.

"Please, Tom," Jeanine coaxed sweetly, "I don't know what this is all about, but Deke's very trustworthy."

Looking very much as though he didn't believe that, Royce went into a room off the kitchen and slammed the door.

Jeanine sat on one foot on a red basket chair and smiled at Duncan. "He's very basic. I like that in a man. Now, what on earth is happening?"

Duncan leaned forward, elbows on his knees, and explained about the aftermath of the wrap party and his lack of memory about it, and the twins with his name on the birth certificate.

She stared at him, blinked, and stared again. "Are you asking me if I was the woman you took upstairs?"

"Yes."

"No." She smiled a little wistfully at him. "I think I'd have loved it then, but no." She made a thoughtful face. "Who else was with us that night? I remember Phoebe and…"

"Yvette Delacroix." He tried to lean back but felt as though his shoulders were pitched forward. He couldn't decide which was more uncomfortable—the situation or the furniture.

"Then it must be Phoebe," Jeanine said with a wince. "Geez. Are you ready for that?"

"It isn't Phoebe." Duncan leaned forward instead. "I've spoken to her."

Jeanine's thoughtful look became troubled. "Well, it can't be Yvette."

"Why not?"

"Her tubes are tied," she said unabashedly. Then, at his vaguely uncomfortable shift of position, she added with an amused smile, "Sorry, but what else do women have to talk about in the wilds of Mexico when all the eligible men are married or too gentlemanly to take advantage of you? We discuss *other* men, clothes, makeup—and our protection."

He nodded, not knowing how to tell her that his unfocused expression wasn't related to her revelation about Yvette, but to the dead end to his search.

"Of course," she added, "women have been known

to conceive after that surgery, but generally I think the chances are pretty slim.''

He sat in confusion another minute, then pushed himself to his feet, suddenly needing movement and fresh air.

''I'm sorry I bothered you, Jeanine,'' he said, as she came to put an arm around him and lead him to the door. ''And I apologize for upsetting your fiancé.''

''He'll be fine.'' She patted his back. ''Don't give up. You'll find her. I know Yvette was still sitting with you after Phoebe and I left. Maybe someone joined you and you just don't remember.'' She laughed lightly and pulled open the door. ''It might have been that gorgeous interpreter. Remember her?''

He frowned in thought.

''Very quiet, very nice, and very, very good. We used her to speak to the extras. Remember how we laughed that a mostly southern California crew had no Spanish-speaking people among them, and that we had to hire someone. Anyway, she always used to look at you as though you were divine.'' She giggled. ''Well, you *are*, but I mean really divine. She had all this glossy dark hair, remember? Big dark eyes, and she was kind of small. She always looked like a Ralph Lauren ad for dressing on safari—even during filming. And the extras, and everyone else for that matter, seemed to love her.''

He stared at the wall in the apartment hallway, trying to call up the face of the woman Jeanine described. But he couldn't. He really hadn't had that much to do with her. But he did remember her hair. It would have been impossible to have met her, even once, and not remember the yards of shiny, rippling hair.

"What was her name?" he asked Jeanine.

She thought. "Um...Angela something. Something kind of ordinary. Gomez? Garcia? Perez! That was it! Angela Perez!"

Angela Perez. Yes. He remembered. But he'd hardly known her. And she'd never given him any indication that she'd had feelings for him.

And that night *had* been about feelings.

He gave Jeanine a hug. "Thanks. I appreciate your not throwing me out when I asked the question."

"Don't be ridiculous. Good luck. When you find this mystery woman, send me a wedding invitation. Or better yet, bring it to the Spielberg set."

He blew her a kiss and headed for his car.

ARIEL WAS NOW absolutely certain that she was being followed. She'd taken the twins to the market for light-bulbs and laundry detergent—two items she'd forgotten when she and Duncan had gone grocery shopping last week—and for a quart of frozen yogurt. She'd rented the old horror film *The Wax Museum,* and she intended to curl up on the sofa and indulge her funky fear quotient.

But by the time she left the supermarket, she was thinking she wouldn't need the movie to scare herself. Someone *was* watching her. She hadn't seen a face, but a smallish man in aviator sunglasses had followed her from the parking lot into the market, and then from aisle to aisle, concealing himself behind an industrial-size box of laundry detergent, then a pyramid stack of cling peaches, then the head of a mop.

Fortunately she met Cliff and Bertie Fisher on her way out of the market. They stopped to admire the babies, and she encouraged conversation with them so that they would walk her out to the car.

Cliff put the bag of groceries in the back for her. Bertie entertained Gabrielle, while Ariel put Michelle into her infant seat.

"We've been enjoying watching the garden take shape," Cliff said. "We're really not snooping, but our bedroom window looks out onto the backyard. The arbor's a nice touch."

Ariel nodded. "I think Duncan intends to plant a white climbing rose up both sides. If you two aren't busy this afternoon," she said, "why don't you come over for coffee. I bought some beads for Olivia's skirt, Bertie, and I've made a little bit of a start on it. I understand you provided the fabric for it."

"I did." Bertie beamed. "And I've just made an upside-down cake." She patted their grocery cart with its giant bags of flour, sugar, and other assorted groceries. "We'll just put this away and be right over."

Cliff came around to hold Ariel's door open for her, and she was able to get away from the market with her neighbors looking on.

She sped home, pulled the station wagon into the garage and locked the door so the car wouldn't be recognized if she was tailed. Then she peered out the low row of narrow windows, watching for a slow-moving vehicle, perhaps, that might be following her.

Satisfied that she'd lost whoever that was, she carried the twins into the house, hurried back for the bag of groceries, then locked herself in and put on the coffee.

Nervousness filled her as she sipped at a cup of coffee before the Fishers arrived. The net was tightening around her; she had to take action—and soon.

If only Cisco would call.

The twins, mercifully, had fallen asleep on the ride home, so she left them in their carriers on the sofa while she paced the room, wishing now that she'd brewed decaf.

It wasn't like her to be jumpy. Jumpy made you stand out, call attention to yourself. In the year she'd been moving from job to job and hiding out, she'd been cool, in charge of her emotions, vigilant.

Now she was a bundle of nerves. But she knew what made the difference. Over the long year, Deke had been a memory she was afraid to believe in. Now she knew that he was more handsome, kinder, infinitely more dear than even her dreams of him.

And at the time she'd left the babies, for their own protection and her father's, she'd known them for only hours. Now they'd woven themselves into her life, and she knew that she could never leave them again, whatever the reason.

So she had to handle this just right, or she stood the chance of losing everything she held dear.

A rap on the back door brought her out of her self-torture and forced her to concentrate on her guests. They stayed for several hours, Cliff watching a ball game on television, while Ariel took Bertie up to her room to show her the dress laid on the foot of the bed.

She'd marked the pattern with tailor's chalk, and in the hours before going to bed each night over the past several days, she'd completed one entire pattern.

"Goodness." Bertie slipped her glasses down her nose and lifted the fabric to study the work. "You have steady hands, Ariel," she praised. Then she added wryly, "Only nine more patterns to go. Olivia will be pleased."

"Do you think so?" Ariel asked. How could the fate of a woman who'd lived before Ariel's own mother had even been born be so important to her, she wondered. But it was. As Harper had said, she'd brought the house a gift. That made her a friend, not a stranger.

"I do." Bertie fluffed out the skirt, then readjusted her glasses and patted Ariel's hand. "We take up each other's causes. That's what women do. Men will fight and die for each other, but we suffer for each other, bear each other's pain. We carry babies for each other, sometimes we even raise them for each other. We're forever connected in a never-ending string, hand in hand down the ages, sharing what we have and what we know."

"But...what do you think she wants from us? Why did she give us the dress?"

Bertie smiled. "Fewer people get married today. And half of those don't stay married. Maybe she was encouraging all you girls to change the statistics."

That was as likely a reason as any Ariel could come up with.

Chapter Eight

Frozen yogurt on top of pineapple upside-down cake was as heavenly a concoction as Ariel had ever tasted. It was midnight, and she was on her second helping and her second viewing of *The Wax Museum*.

She'd bathed and changed the babies, and had played with them until Gabrielle yawned mightily and Michelle got cranky. She rocked them together, singing *"No Sé Tu,"* a song a patron with a guitar had been singing in the cantina that fateful night. She was careful never to sing it when Duncan was around.

She had brought the portable crib downstairs to Peg and Charlie's room so that she could put the babies down and still be close enough to hear them. Then she had put on her movie and had been lolling on the sofa ever since, except for the occasional trip to the kitchen for more tea, more cake, more frozen yogurt.

The sugar high seemed to help alleviate her fears and make the whole surreal picture in which she found herself more rosy.

When the credits rolled for the second time, she was no longer able to keep her eyes open. Rather than try to carry the crib and the babies upstairs, however, she simply brought a blanket down and curled up on the sofa.

She fell asleep thinking about having frozen yogurt on pineapple upside-down cake for breakfast.

SHE AWOKE WITH A START into complete darkness, her heart pounding. She sat up, waiting for a sensory report to her brain on what had awakened her.

She was aware of the upholstered back of the sofa right beside her and remembered that she'd chosen to sleep downstairs rather than to move the twins.

But what had disturbed her? She'd had no dreams, so it had to be something real.

The babies weren't crying. There was no sound on the street.

She put a hand to her thudding heart and knew that something had frightened her subconscious, shaking her to awareness.

She tossed the blanket aside and moved carefully around the coffee table to check on the babies. Maybe some instinct about them had prodded her awake.

She went through the kitchen and into the bedroom, flipping the hallway light on so that she could see into the crib without the glare of the overhead.

To her relief, both babies were fast asleep, apparently just fine. She put a hand to each one, felt the gentle rise and fall of easy breathing.

And then she heard the noise through the window screen. It was the plague of every adventure movie, and every woman alone in a dark house: the snapping of a twig that meant movement.

And it was just outside the bedroom window.

Every fear she'd had earlier in the day of being

watched returned to accelerate her heartbeat even further. She brought both hands to her mouth.

She hadn't lost whoever had been following her. He'd just been waiting outside for her to be alone— for the neighborhood to be asleep—before making his move.

Then her protective instincts kicked in. Moving stealthily so that she wouldn't be heard outside, she pulled the crib away from the window and turned it sideways behind the dresser. She reached into the hallway and flipped off the light.

The sound outside was moving toward the front of the house. She closed the bedroom door and ran to the kitchen for the phone. She dialed 911, and as the line rang she heard movement at the front window.

She waited through another ring, her heartbeat choking her, whispering, "Answer! Answer! Answer!"

But the only answer was the squeak and thud of the old window as it was pushed up, resisted the movement, and was pushed up again. Terror trickled down her spine.

Accepting that she was now the last line of defense between the intruder and her twins, she left the phone dangling and reached for the broom standing up in a corner. Holding it like a lance, handle foremost, she headed through the dining room at a run, aiming for the dark shape she saw emerge through the open window.

She heard herself screaming.

Bracing herself for the impact of wood and bone, Ariel ran with a ruthless determination that surprised even her.

So it was with stunned disbelief that she realized a

second later that she'd missed her mark altogether. She heard a clatter as the broom went flying out of her hands and she, herself, collided, hitting bone in her chin and stomach.

The already-black world went blacker still as air left her lungs and she felt herself sliding, sliding...

But her brain held on to the threat to her babies and herself and she noisily dragged in air, trying to marshal energy to push against the body with which she'd collided.

"Ariel!" Duncan's voice said sharply. "What are you doing? It's me!"

Duncan? *Duncan.*

Oh, mercy. How was she going to explain this reaction? So the threat wasn't physical, but now even more serious than she'd thought.

She abandoned the struggle and let herself slide.

But she never made it to the floor; she was lifted up and carried to the sofa. As the glaring overhead light went on, she turned away with a moan.

Duncan sat on the edge of the sofa and turned her over, his hands running gently over the silk nightshirt that covered her, as though trying to assess damage.

"I'm sorry, Ariel." He touched a finger to her chin that was already sore from its impact with his shoulder.

She winced, and he did, too.

"I had no idea you'd still be awake," he explained. "God, you're going to have a bruise there. I had the new car key, but I'd left my house key on the old ring, and both doors were locked."

It's all right, she told herself. *He doesn't know I expected a threat from elsewhere, he just thinks I thought he was a prowler. It's okay. I don't have to explain anything.*

She sat up, a hand to her reeling head. "I rented a movie," she said feebly, "and watched it twice. It was late and the twins were sleeping so soundly, I...I thought I'd just sleep down here...rather than have to carry them upstairs."

"Very sensible."

"You said you might not be home until morning."

He nodded. "But I got to see her right away."

He would expect her to ask the question, but he was leaning over her so solicitously, stroking her cheek...and besides, it would have been a lie.

Apparently presuming she didn't think it was her place to ask, he volunteered the answer. "It wasn't her. And she says it can't be Yvette Delacroix. Seems she has permanent protection in place."

"Ah," she said softly.

He nodded grimly. "And I just felt this urgent need to get back to you and the twins."

She heard that. *You* and the twins.

"That's why you heard me turning doorknobs and raising windows in the middle of the night."

She tried to answer, but a sob blocked the sound. He didn't look at all surprised—but *she* was. She'd thought she had it together.

But there he was, big and solid and...home. And it hadn't been Suarez out there at all, just Duncan wanting to get back to her and the babies.

And there were all these ugly secrets she was hiding of which he had no idea, and she knew he would lose that sweet, sympathetic, guilty look in his eyes when he found them out.

"Now, don't cry," he pleaded, taking her into his

arms. "It's all right. Everything's fine. Just go back to whatever you were dreaming about when I woke you up."

"I wasn't dreaming," she whispered.

"Okay, then let's plant a dream in your mind," he said rubbing gently up and down her back. "And maybe your subconscious will take it over when you fall asleep."

She leaned into him, loving the touch of his fingertips against her—even through the silk of her shirt. She could remember the time when there'd been nothing between his fingers and her warm skin, and she trembled at the sensory image.

She knew that he felt the little shudder against him, and he held her closer, apparently horrified that he'd so frightened her.

"I don't think you can seed dreams," she said with a frail laugh.

"Sure you can," he insisted briskly. "Where would you want to be in this dream?"

She hesitated a moment, then she replied quietly, "I guess…right here."

"In this house?"

"Yes."

"Well, that's not very inventive, but okay. Where in this house?"

She readjusted her cheek against his chest and tightened her grip on him. "Your room," she replied. Her voice was soft but very clear.

HE TOOK A MOMENT to absorb that information and accept the challenge that came with it. He took another moment to decide whether to back away from it, or to follow where it led.

Then he realized in the next moment, when she sighed against him, that he didn't really have a choice. He moved one hand to the back of her head and gently tipped it back.

"You don't like *your* room?" he asked into her deep brown eyes, fear still visible in their depths. He wanted so much to banish that.

"No," she whispered.

He drew a shallow breath. "Why not?"

"You're not there," she replied instantly, her eyes filled with that frank, familiar look he often saw in her when he was inclined to back away.

But tonight was different. Tonight he'd lost his lead and had no clear direction where his life was going.

And her gentle desire was like a beacon. *Come to me. Come to* me.

A loud rapping on the front door brought Ariel upright, and Duncan to his feet. The sound was followed by the appearance of a blue-clad leg through the open window.

"Oh, the police!" Ariel said, running past him to the door, unlatching it and pulling it open.

Finding the will to move after those languid and promising few moments, Duncan went to the window to help a second officer through.

"I left the phone off the hook—" her cheeks were pink as she explained to the officers and to Duncan "—I thought he was an intruder, but he's really my employer. He forgot his key. 911 didn't answer and I knew I had to do something, so I left the phone dangling, thinking maybe if worse came to worst you could hear that there was a problem and somehow trace the call. Which you seem to have done. Oh, God. Excuse me."

She ran into the kitchen, presumably to replace the telephone receiver.

Duncan met the officers' suspicious stares.

"Would you like to see some ID?" he offered. "I know it looks—"

"You're Bruce Willis!" one of the officers interrupted.

Duncan laughed. "No, I'm—"

"Steven Seagal!"

Before Duncan could tell him that he was wrong, the second officer studied him with a pensive frown. "No, he was the bad guy in those movies. Ah, ah…" He snapped his fingers, trying to come up with a name.

"Duncan McKeon," Duncan said, reaching out to shake hands. "Sorry to call you out in the middle of the night, but it's nice to know you're out there."

While the first officer stepped aside to answer a call on his radio, the second apologized for the delay. "Our response time is usually much better than this, but it took us a while to track you down. Fortunately for all of us, you weren't a prowler after all."

"Right."

"So, you're here to make a movie?"

"No, I'm here on vacation," he replied, explaining briefly about buying the house with his brothers.

Ariel joined them again, still flushed and apologetic.

"Not a problem," the second officer insisted. "We like calls that turn out to be nothing." He turned to his companion, who'd turned off the receiver on his collar. "Another call?"

The first officer grinned. "Yeah. The sarge wants a burger on our way back to the com center." He turned to Duncan. "Nice to meet you, Mr. McKeon."

Duncan nodded and shook hands with one officer, then the other. "My pleasure. Sorry we troubled you."

The radio crackled again and the officers said goodnight and went out to their car.

Duncan closed and locked the door behind them, then closed and locked the window.

He turned to Ariel, sure the officers' sudden arrival would have cooled the ardent urgency he'd seen in her eyes.

But she was right behind him, that same look lighting her gaze, her arms open to him.

"All right," he said, putting a hand to the back of her neck and drawing her toward him. "Let's make that dream come true."

She met his mouth greedily, standing on tiptoe to wrap her arms around his neck.

He'd played this kind of scene so many times that the very unromantic details of doing it for film sometimes invaded the personal pleasure of doing it for real—remembering not to conceal the actress's face, to guard his own expression, to move with grace.

But not this time. Ariel's kiss made him forget everything—that he was skilled at this, that she probably wasn't, that he should try to answer a few more questions for himself before he proceeded.

She was eager for him. He was desperate for her. That was all he knew.

While she planted kisses along his jawline and behind his ear, he pressed her to him, a little alarmed suddenly by how fragile she felt.

Then again, she had a leg wrapped around his and was hanging from his neck, so he guessed she had reservoirs of strength and stamina he didn't suspect.

With one hand he lifted the silk nightshirt, and ran the other over the soft flare of her bottom.

She groaned against his earlobe and tightened her hold on him.

"Upstairs," Duncan whispered urgently.

"Yes," she replied, managing to draw her mouth—but not her body—away from him. "The babies…are in your parents' room."

He finally set her on her feet. "We'll each take one," he said, pulling her back for another kiss. "And I'll carry the crib."

"Okay."

The plan took less than five minutes to execute. Luckily, neither Michelle nor Gabrielle fluttered an eyelash. Duncan set them up in a corner of the room away from the draft of the window, then turned out the lights.

Then he caught Ariel's hand and led her to the bed, falling back on it and bringing her with him.

He pulled the silk shirt off her and tossed it blindly behind him. For long moments, he explored every silken line of her, traced the curves, mapped the hollows, then returned again to memorize her every gasp and sigh.

Every doubt Ariel had ever had that he would be hers again vanished with the possessive quality of his touch. She rose to it, turned to it, reveled in it.

She lifted his cotton sweater and T-shirt, and strung kisses along the jut of his ribs. He pulled his shirts the rest of the way off.

She unfastened his belt, unzipped his slacks and pulled them and his briefs down and off. He was propped up on his elbows and she tried to push him back, but he caught her arms instead, pulled her down beside him and leaned to tuck her under him.

He took her mouth again, then bent her knee to stroke up the back of her thigh, over her hip, then down again and inside her.

She felt as though her blood effervesced.

Pleasure came upon her swiftly and suddenly, just a sparkle of sensation at first that turned in an instant into a conflagration.

Duncan delighted in her body's response to him, then forgot his gentle observations a moment later when her small hand closed over him and his proud satisfaction turned to profound humility.

He rose over her and entered her, loving the little sigh of satisfaction with which she welcomed him.

Then her body enclosed him and he seemed to lose all power to sustain observer status. With the tender touch of her small hands and the eager response of her slender body, she banished every negative thought he'd ever had, every black cloud that had ever hovered overhead, every fear, every concern, every suggestion of anger.

She loved him with a generosity that was almost heart-rending in its perfection.

Their bodies turned several times in their lovemaking, he uppermost, then she, then he again.

He lay on his back as the wild spiral of sex and emotion began to slowly uncoil, as she collapsed on top of him, her body still enfolding him, and rubbed her forehead and hair against his cheek as though she were some feline goddess.

And that was when he began to remember.

When the notion first struck him—more sensation

than fact, too thinly structured to even coalesce into an idea—he tried to discard it as outrageous.

But sensation crowded upon sensation and he realized that that was all the memory of that night in Mexico had been—no fact, simply one sensory impression pressed against another until it became real enough to identify.

And he did so now.

Skin like silk, flower-petal kisses, a touch so gentle its beauty almost caused pain. Cool sheets, a fragrant ocean breeze.

All that was missing was the sweep of long hair against his body, and the *mariachis* in the cantina downstairs.

The truth pinned him to the pillow and struck him repeatedly with the blunt object of his own stupidity.

Ariel was the woman from the night in the cantina.

Ariel was the mother of his babies.

Chapter Nine

Duncan's first thought was self-recriminatory. As Ariel lay quietly atop him, recovering from their love-making, he wondered why he hadn't been able to identify her in the light of day.

Ariel Bonneau was Angela Perez.

As he recalled, he really hadn't had that much to do with the translator, except that once he'd interceded when the leading man had come on to her and wouldn't take no for an answer.

After that she'd smile at him when she saw him—but that had been it.

He did remember the clouds of dark hair Jeanine had spoken of, and that he'd thought her beautiful enough to star in the film rather than being behind the scenes.

Ariel was Angela without makeup, and with all that luxurious hair cropped off.

He felt like Perry White and Jimmy Olson and all the other residents of Metropolis who never connected Clark Kent to Superman because of a simple pair of eyeglasses.

Once he got over feeling inexcusably dense, he had to deal with confusion. Why hadn't Ariel/Angela simply come to him when she found herself pregnant? Why had she left the babies at the hospital and run away? Where had she been all this time? Why was she playing this masquerade with him? And how the hell had Dori gotten mixed up with her?

The litany of questions with no apparent answers— at least no forgivable ones—turned the confusion to an anger so strong he felt it radiating to his extremities. But the hot center of it beat right in his heart.

Ariel raised her head from his chest suddenly, as though she'd sensed the change in him. She looked into his eyes in the darkness, her own sheened with the moonlight from the window.

She put a soothing hand to his brow—her fingertips creating exactly the touch that had textured his dreams since Mexico. The touch that had made him believe in a love that was turning out to be as unreal as any love scene played out in front of a camera.

That was when the villain in him surfaced. Because the villain was real. It wasn't simply a persona he donned when the director shouted "Action." It was who he was, deep down.

Oh, he loved his parents and his siblings, and his friends. But on a level he usually kept buried, he didn't really believe in anything else. That was probably why he could play one bastard after another so convincingly. It was his theory that villainy wasn't so much in the evil intent as in the lack of belief in good intent. And considering the success of his career, he was right.

"Are you regretting this?" she asked in a small voice.

He made the cold-blooded decision as she stroked his temple that until she decided to tell him the truth, he could play this game better than she could. And he could destroy Harper's Aunt Gracie's theory that all his villains had a good side.

At this moment, he was as bad as bad got.

"Of course not." He ran a hand the length of her spine, tracing the curve of her hip and lingering there. "How could I regret you?" Knowing that a good performance was in the subtleties, he pinched her bottom and, with just the right amount of selfish conviction, added, "You're everything a man dreams about finding to light up a summer break."

Her eyes were uncertain. He could see that she didn't think he could mean what he suggested—that this hadn't been about her at all, but simply about *it*.

He ran his fingers up through her short hair, then smoothed it back down again. "Warm," he said with a lascivious self-satisfaction in his voice and manner that he'd perfected as Devlin Cross, "inviting, willing. And more quick to learn than one would expect of an ex-nun."

She sat up on him now, her distress deepening. "Duncan..."

"Don't worry about the parts you didn't quite get. We'll work on those before you go home. In fact, we can polish up your—"

She gave him a violent shove and got to her feet.

For an instant she quivered in the darkness right beside him, a small, wispy image in the shadows, the curve of breast, stomach and thigh highlighted by moonglow. Then she snatched up the nightshirt he'd thrown to the carpet earlier and with another last, horrified look at him, ran from the room.

He felt good. *So* good.

It was probably the cappuccino he'd picked up on the drive home that was giving him a headache.

ARIEL SAT ON the carpet in her bathroom and sobbed with fury, the bathroom and the bedroom doors closed so that she couldn't be heard. She wouldn't give Duncan the satisfaction of knowing how much he'd hurt her.

He'd used her as a summer distraction? She couldn't believe that. He'd made love to her with the perfection every mature woman dreamed of—with the tenderness of a gentleman, and the passion of a rogue. He'd seemed completely captivated by her and yet possessively confident of her love for him.

How *could* that have been simply about sex?

She thought hard as the tears fell and sorrow welled in her.

The man who'd stood between her and an intoxicated and over-amorous actor on a Mexican beach would never take advantage of the hired help. And the man who'd planted the twins in her that delicious night wasn't capable of thinking of a woman as an object. He'd been too caring, too considerate, too…involved.

Tonight's behavior had to be prompted by something else.

Her sobs quieted as a possibility occurred to her. Could he know the truth, and be punishing her for her trickery?

The notion fanned her fury. But the more she thought about it, the more she realized that *he* had far more to be angry about than she did.

But if he knew, wouldn't he have confronted her? Wouldn't he have a hundred questions for which he

would demand answers? Wouldn't he be anxious to
verbally pound her with his opinion of a woman who
would take advantage of a man under the influence of
prescription drugs and champagne? Who would have
his babies without telling him, abandon them, hide
from him, and then move in on him pretending to be
someone else?

His response didn't make sense.

And the worst part of all was that now, every time
she looked at him, she would wonder whether he
knew. And if he didn't know now, her questioning and
guilty looks would certainly betray her.

She got to her feet and paced the small room, thinking. She had to stay here to await word from Cisco.
Then she would be free to have it all out with Duncan,
or to take her babies and go, if that was what he
wanted.

But until then, she had to bide her time.

Presuming he *didn't* know about her, how could she
spend every hour in his company without looking
guilty or put-upon?

As she paced, she caught her reflection in the mirror—and it came to her. She would do it by being a
bit of an actor herself.

So far she'd played the shy but capable nanny attracted to the master of the house. All she had to do
was take that up a notch and become the nanny who'd
completely succumbed to the master's touch and was
now helplessly in love. So when he saw love and guilt
in her eyes, it would belong there.

And when this was all over…she would give him
a right to the jaw.

Ariel washed her face, clearing away most evidence
of her tears. She smoothed her nightshirt, spritzed on

a little floral fragrance, squared her shoulders and looked her reflection in the eye.

"All you have to do," she told herself, "is convince him that you don't mind being his summer fling." She watched her own gaze turn wicked and accepted that part of herself with a tilt of her chin. He wasn't the only one who could play a villain. She had a trace of villainy, too. And she'd come by hers quite naturally. "And maybe I'll teach him a thing or two along the way."

Duncan lay on his side, facing the bright half-moon visible through the window, when he heard the sound of soft footsteps on the hardwood floor.

What now? he wondered.

The mattress took another weight, and a small, supple body curled up against his back. Then a pair of very cold feet found warmth by burrowing against him just below his knees.

An arm came around his waist. "You gave me a dream," she whispered in his ear. "I guess I can do the same for you. I know I have a lot to learn…but later I'll be able to say I was taught by Duncan McKeon." She kissed behind his ear. "Maybe tomorrow we can go skinny-dipping. Good night."

Heaven help him, Duncan thought, as she snuggled against him. He'd wandered onto a Stephen King set.

THEY DID NOT GO skinny-dipping.

Duncan went to buy lumber to build a fence around the backyard and was gone for hours.

Ariel fed and changed the babies. Then she propped each one against pillows on the sofa on either side of her and talked to them about their father, while she worked beads onto Olivia's skirt.

"I'm doing my best to keep us together," she told them. "And I think it's all going to come out right. Of course, I've been telling myself that since my mother died and my father drafted me into the—" she lowered her voice "—the *business*." She cleared her throat and stitched a bugle bead in place. "You have to learn this sooner or later. Your grandfather and your uncles and your…I don't know what he is…second cousin, or cousin twice removed, something like that. Anyway, he's *my* cousin. Well, they're all cat burglars." She sighed, looked from one baby to the other, and gave them big smiles. They smiled back, cheering her considerably.

"I don't think there are that many of them anymore, but your grandfather's the best. Actually, I was pretty good, too, except that he never let me touch anything they stole. I just got inside and let everyone else in. But that was when I was just a girl. I quit to go to school and your grandfather was very upset with me."

She held the fabric up, pleased to see the third pattern taking shape. But thoughts of her father, and the relationship she'd never quite been able to repair since that day, brought a frown to her forehead.

"Your grandpa's really a very good man who cares a lot about the people he grew up with in Mexico. They're very poor and no one really cares about them but him. Everything he steals goes to build things for them—a water system, a school, a small hospital. He does good work, but stealing from other people is wrong.

"I want you to get to know him, but we're all in kind of a mess right now and he's hiding from the police. I'm trying to find a way for him to give himself up, but I think he's going to have to go to jail—and that breaks my heart. But I'm just not going to have you grow up with felons for relatives.''

Michelle jabbered her approval. Gabrielle kicked and battled the air.

''I've spent my entire life trying to keep my family together though we disagreed completely on how to live our lives,'' Ariel went on. ''And now it seems I'm going to have to do the same with us. The situation has put your father and me on opposite sides and it's going to take some fast talking to get us together. But that's my plan. I want you to know that. But if all fails, we're out of here together—the three of us.''

The sound of a big motor in the driveway brought Ariel to her feet to peer through the front window. Duncan had arrived, followed by a large truck with the Dancer's Beach Builders Supply logo on the door. Lengths of lumber protruded from the bed, and bundles of pickets filled it.

Ariel put the babies in their carriers and brought them into the kitchen with her, while Duncan supervised the storing of his supplies in the garage.

''I think your dad's planning a big project so he can avoid me,'' she told the babies as she placed them on the counter. She went to the refrigerator for sliced turkey, lettuce and tomato. ''But he doesn't know that I refuse to be avoided. Watch closely. Every woman is a tactician at heart.'' She put the groceries down, then went to hold and squeeze each little hand. ''Not a trickster, but a tactician. There's an important difference, so pay attention.''

DUNCAN COULDN'T GET a moment's peace. He'd brought fencing home a week ago in order to have a valid reason to be out in the yard while Ariel was in the house, but the fates—and Ariel—were conspiring against him.

At intervals she brought him coffee or iced tea and a piece of coffee cake she'd baked, or a cookie Bertie had brought over. She carried the twins out every lunchtime and set the picnic table, then served an elaborate lunch.

Then she sat across from him and chatted while they ate, stretching the meal out to include a second and sometimes third cup of tea or coffee.

Dinners were hearty and delicious and always followed by dessert—things he hadn't had in years such as three-layer cake, or Dutch apple pie, or brownies *à la mode*.

He was grateful that he had physically taxing work, though he was beginning to wonder if the calories consumed weren't outdistancing those expended.

The long evenings were the worst. After dinner he and Ariel played with the babies, who were growing so lively and responsive that he kept expecting them to speak.

It was more than clear that Ariel loved them. He often remembered the first time she saw them—or at least the first time she saw them in *his* presence. She had been eager to touch, then tried to check the gesture—maybe afraid it would somehow give her away—then finally seemed to give in as though she simply couldn't help herself.

Now her expression was always filled with wonder and pride when she looked at them. And she had a way with them that could only be maternal. There were moments when he couldn't quiet Michelle, but he would hand her to Ariel, and, with a few whispers and a little rocking, the baby would settle down.

Trying to establish a routine, they put the twins to bed at nine o'clock, and though there was an occasional fussy night, they were usually asleep by nine-fifteen for a good eight hours.

Then Ariel would make popcorn, find something on television, and snuggle up to him on the sofa. She made any neutrality on his part impossible.

He would tell himself that tonight he'd do nothing more than put an arm around her, to support his role as lascivious employer. That he wouldn't let himself be lured into anything else.

But she would lean into him, look up at him to share her laughter or the drama of the moment, or cling to him when the drama became tense or frightening.

He would hold her a little closer and before he knew it they were sprawled and wrapped around each other on the sofa and barely made it to the bed before the serious lovemaking was under way.

Things were not going the way he'd planned, but he was determined to wait her out.

She was going to reveal herself to *him*.

ARIEL DID HER BEST to keep up the live-for-the-moment appearance of the role she'd assumed, but she was certain she would never win an award for it from the Academy of Motion Picture Arts and Sciences. In fact, she had a feeling she would never even have been nominated.

Though she tried to cover with cheerful chattiness and lots of eyelash batting, her interpretation of the naughty nanny lacked a certain conviction.

She'd had it in the beginning, and coupled with anger at his attitude—feigned or not—it was a pretty powerful thing.

But she began to lose it when his reaction was luke-warm. Oh, his physical response to her was hot and eager, but all the qualities with which he'd approached it before—both in Mexico and the night she'd mistaken him for one of Suarez's men—was missing.

Her efforts dissembled when she began to realize that he couldn't be faking that part. His tenderness and his compassion were woven into his being; he wouldn't be able to turn them off. So, either he wasn't at all impressed with her now that he'd made love to her half a dozen times, or he *did* know about her and this was part of his own retribution.

Either way, she felt demoralized and distinctly second class.

But the pretense had to continue. So she had to find a way to put a little more substance into her performance.

Duncan had two sides of the fence up now, with only one more to go. But they woke up one Thursday morning to rain pounding on the roof and slashing against the windows.

"Oh!" Ariel said, delighted. She leapt out of bed and into her robe. "A summer storm. You can't work on the fence in the rain. You'll have to stay in with us all day!"

Duncan thought quickly. "There's lots I can do in the garage."

She ignored him. "We'll picnic. I'll fry chicken and make mojos, and we have corn on the cob and three-bean salad. Then we can make sugar-cinnamon twists."

He turned over in bed, as she belted her robe and leaned into the crib where one of the babies was awake and greeting her with high-pitched gurgles.

"That doesn't compute, Ariel," he said, burrowing his cheek in the pillow. It was getting harder and harder to sleep with her curled up beside him. It wasn't sexual frustration, because she insisted on relieving him of that every night. It was some emotional frustration that was pushing him farther and farther to the outside edge of his patience and tolerance.

He wanted to know the truth. But he didn't want to coerce it out of her. He wanted her to tell him. He wanted to know that some part of the memory of that night that he'd held with reverence for a year remained intact.

"We can't picnic in the rain." He pointed a hand over his head in the direction of the crib. "Not good for the girls."

"Of course we can." She leapt onto the bed on her knees, and nipped his ear. "We'll do it on the living room floor."

He turned his face away. "Oh, that'll be cozy."

Undaunted, she propped her hands on his shoulders and leaned over him to look into his face. "It will. Trust me. And you'll love the sugar-cinnamon twists."

He was going to lose this. He could see it coming. "What the hell is that, anyway?" he asked crossly.

"It's croissant dough dipped in melted butter and rolled in cinnamon sugar. You wrap it around a stick and put it in the fire."

All *right*. "Well," he said, averting his face again, "unless you intend to start a fire in the middle of the sofa, it can wait for better weather."

"Good Lord," she said with good-natured impatience. "We'll build a fire in the woodstove." She swatted his backside through the blanket. "Come on.

I'll make a camp breakfast. Bacon and eggs and hot-cakes.''

She picked up a squealing Michelle and placed her on the mattress beside him, while she kissed Gabrielle and put her to her shoulder. "Will you watch Michelle while I set up the playpen in the kitchen? If I'm going to be in there all morning, I don't want them to have to be in their infant seats."

And that was how he lost the battle against a "family" day that he was sure was going to push him over the edge. Over the last week and a half, Ariel had become the epitome of the cozy homemaker, and it was driving him insane.

Not because he didn't like it, but because he did. For a man who spent much of his time on a movie set, and the rest of it in a comfortable—but hardly cozy—mansion in Malibu, cozy had a dimension he'd thought he'd forgotten, except when he got together with his family.

It made him feel warm and contented and filled with goodwill. It seemed to evaporate his grievances, to shine up his memories so that he forgot a lot of things he was mad about in his life—or put them in a different perspective.

It made him imagine the twins growing up and spending summers in the shelter of this warm and wonderful house, surrounded by the love of his parents and his siblings and their families. And it made him remember his own childhood.

It made him remember Donovan.

It made him remember that though he hadn't been able to save Donovan's life, he'd laughed with him when he'd still been strong enough to laugh. And he'd sat with him for hours on end.

It made him remember that before Donovan had slipped away, he'd told Duncan that he loved him.

Duncan realized with deep alarm that Ariel's cozy atmosphere was taking the villain out of him.

Duncan braced up on his elbows, brought Michelle between his arms, and lay her on his pillow.

"Your mother's driving me nuts," he said. "But you know that. She probably drives you crazy, too, with that endless good cheer and her quick and simple solutions to every domestic crisis. Are we really ready for a picnic on the living room floor?"

Michelle grinned broadly and kicked him in the throat, signifying, he presumed, that she was.

And damn it, so was he. If he ignored what it did to his emotional self, it was one of the nicest days he'd had in years.

She brought breakfast out to him in the living room, where he watched an old Cary Grant movie, unintentionally studying technique. Duncan had never considered Grant a really brilliant actor, but the man moved with a grace and style worth emulating.

Ariel fed Gabrielle, while Michelle talked nonstop as she lay beside Duncan on the sofa. Then he fed Michelle so Ariel could eat.

Ariel cooked most of the morning, preparing the chicken, peeling and slicing potatoes for mojos. The room was soon filled with the most wonderful aromas. He read the paper at the kitchen table, the babies in the playpen beside him entertained by the teddy bear mobile he'd attached to the side. George Strait's voice wafted gently from a small disc player he'd bought for the kitchen, at pleasant odds with the calliope-like sound of the mobile.

A sudden cloudburst threw rain against the window,

and he looked up to watch it sheet down the pane. But his gaze was snared by Ariel at the counter, singing along with the music, turning instinctively to check on the babies, who were seemingly content in their little mesh world.

He experienced a stab of emotion so great it stole his breath. This was what he wanted in his life.

The realization gave him a shock. How could he want her so desperately? She'd abandoned his babies and lied to him. Was he some kind of masochist?

She turned to him at that moment and must have seen all those thoughts in his eyes.

"What?" she asked anxiously.

He tried to think. "Um—" he indicated the paper he read "—the economic situation in Russia. It's grim."

She smiled, unable to hide her relief. "But there's nothing you can do about that today, so don't let it get you down. You're supposed to be relaxing. You know, I was thinking, when the fence is finished, you should get the girls a puppy."

He shook his head. "Not a good idea. If I take the girls with me on the set, what would I do with the dog? Or if I leave the girls home, my housekeeper would have to take care of him, and that's not fair to her or the dog."

Now she was the one who looked as though she had the weight of the world on her shoulders, he thought. His response had been a deliberate ploy on his part to remind her that the way things were—or the way she *thought* they were—she would be going home eventually, and he'd be going back to work. His intention was to make her confess her game.

But she didn't. She just looked devastated and went back to cutting up potatoes.

He told himself that it was her own fault. If she'd been honest with him, he wouldn't have to needle her.

He went back to his paper.

When everything was ready, she moved the coffee table away from the sofa and spread a blanket in the middle of the room. She brought pillows out and set two places, then carried one baby to the blanket and came back for the other.

Duncan carried the playpen into the living room and put the babies back in it. Then Ariel handed him a large basket covered with a tea towel.

He studied it in amazement. "A picnic on the living room floor complete with picnic *basket?*"

"Of course. Props are important to set the scene." She followed him with a bottle of wine and a corkscrew. "I'd have thought an actor would know that."

He put the basket down in the middle of the Stuart-plaid blanket. "I didn't even know we *owned* a basket."

"Bertie brought cookies and a bundt cake in it the other day. Plates are in the bottom under the chicken."

A gray light filled the room as rain outside continued to fall in earnest. It might have been February, except for the temperature.

Ariel disappeared into his parents' bedroom and returned with a potted silk ficus—about four feet tall—that inhabited one corner. She placed it just out of reach of his right elbow. Then she put a disc in the disc player, and soft violin music began to fill the room.

"Violins at a picnic?" he asked. "Shouldn't it be guitars?"

"Gypsies don't play guitars." When they were seated cross-legged in the middle of the blanket, she reached into the basket for a napkin to place over his knee.

"Gypsies picnic?" He was beginning to enjoy this already, but he felt obliged to tease her. "I thought they lived and ate in those cool wagons?"

She gave him a quelling look. "They're not picnicking gypsies. They're a little band of musicians hired to play at *our* picnic somewhere on a hillside in Yorkshire."

She took one of the plates he'd removed from the basket and balanced it on his knee. "We live there."

He frowned, steadying the plate, as she placed on it a succulent piece of fried chicken breast. "We're farmers?"

She put a piece on her own plate. "No. You've just inherited a dukedom, and I'm the catch of the London season. But we couldn't find time to talk with all those people around and one frivolous event after another, so you've brought me to your country estate to talk things over."

She put an ear of corn on his plate, a spoonful of three-bean salad and a biscuit.

"What things?" he asked.

"The marriage contract," she replied airily, adding all the same things to her plate. "You want to know what I'm bringing to our union."

Duncan propped his back against a chair. "That's venal of me."

"No, you're just a product of the times we live in and of your family obligations." She handed him the bottle of wine and the corkscrew. Then she grinned.

"And my family's pretty scandalous. You have your reputation to think of."

"I see." He opened the wine with a skill he'd developed while playing Owen Farr, the reprobate son of a powerful banker. So maybe he *was* equipped to play the role she'd assigned him after all. "So what *are* you bringing to this union?"

"Our vast estates in America." She held their glasses out, while he poured. "And you're wondering if you should chuck all the confining obligations of your position here and take over my place in Virginia."

"I can't leave my people—" he righted and corked the bottle, then set it aside "—and let the land fall to ruin. I can't be venal *and* selfish."

She smiled broadly and toasted him with her glass. "That's probably why I love you. And why I've offered to sell the lands in America so that you can restore the church, build a school, repair the cottages, and all those other selfless things you want to do."

"Excellent solution." He clicked his glass with hers and drank. "And I've accepted your scandalous family?"

She pulled a small plastic container out of the basket and concentrated on it with more seriousness than it seemed to deserve. She poured three green olives out of it onto his plate.

"Actually, I've kept a lot of the details from you," she said, now applying the same concentration to fitting the lid back on the container, "because I'm afraid of losing you."

He knew that there was a second level to this conversation. But what was she telling him? "Maybe you should have more faith in me," he said.

"My past is worse than you can imagine."

"Maybe you should have more faith in me," he repeated.

"I guess I'm afraid." She finally dropped the container back in the basket. "I've never had so much to lose before."

"I think you'd be more likely to lose me because of lies or secrets, than because of past mistakes or whatever you're keeping from me. Certainly I've made a few of my own."

She took a sip of wine and looked into his face, her lips parting, her eyes urgent—as though the truth were just a breath away.

Time hung suspended while they held each other's glance—he with quiet patience, she with a desperate need he could see but couldn't define.

Then she closed her mouth, took another sip of wine and shook her head, laughing stiffly. "Maybe I'll just run away with one of the gypsies."

Acutely disappointed, he maintained a calm expression and broke his biscuit in half. "Then I'd have to chase you down and bring you back."

Eyebrows arched in surprise, she handed him a covered bowl of butter. "You'd do that?"

"Thank you." He accepted the butter, then the knife she handed him. "Well, if we're on this hillside talking marriage, presumably I'm deeply in love with you. So there's no way I'm losing you. You either come back with me peacefully, or I waste the gypsy and you come back draped over my saddle." That multilayered little fantasy delivered, he looked up with a grin. "I *do* have a horse?"

She nodded, her expression part confusion, part longing. "Your family raises them for racing."

"Well, there you have it. You can't elude me for long when I'm following you on a horse bred for racing. And if you love me enough to have considered my proposal in the first place, then the gypsy's just an error in judgment and you want to come back to me anyway."

She stared at him, clearly unsure if he was tuned into the double entendres. He maintained a look of innocence as he took a bite of biscuit.

"I'm sure that's it," she finally said, then turned her attention to her meal.

He congratulated himself on a well-played skirmish in their battle of wits. It was an ongoing thing, however, attacking him on all fronts. And while he'd managed to sidestep the issue of a dog, he wasn't as agile when it came to the cat.

Or rather, when the cat came to them.

The twins were asleep in the playpen, and Duncan was helping Ariel clean up after their picnic. It was late afternoon and the continuing storm darkened the day outside, creating shadows in corners of the rooms.

But the house was warm. Ariel had asked him to build a fire in the woodstove so that they could make sugar-cinnamon things when they'd finished cleaning up.

Duncan heard the high, plaintive sound, just as Ariel's head came up and her hands stilled on the frypan she'd been scrubbing. Thinking one of the babies was awake, or had cried out in her sleep, he went into the living room to investigate. He found both babies asleep, curled up together, little hands entwined.

When he returned to the kitchen, Ariel was awaiting his report.

"They're fine," he said, puzzled. "Both sound asleep."

Then the sound came again, a little higher this time and a little more plaintive. He leaned over the counter to look out the kitchen window, and, seeing nothing, went to the back door and pulled it open.

A soaked and scrawny black cat clung to the outside of the screen door, pea-green eyes desperate.

"Oh!" Ariel cried sympathetically.

Looking like the famous "Hang in there!" illustration, the cat meowed at Duncan, eyes enormous in a pointed face that was all black except for a white mustache. This time there was demand in the sound as well as anguish. *I deserve to be fed!* the cat seemed to say. *And a warm corner to sleep in wouldn't be rejected, either!*

Duncan pushed the door open and walked around it to free the cat. He wrapped his hand around the thin stomach and lifted him off the door, cradling his hind end in his other hand. The cat hung there passively. Duncan took him inside, and Ariel hurried to dry him off with a wad of paper towels.

"Does he have a collar?" she asked anxiously.

"Nope. Nothing."

"All *right*," she said triumphantly. "He's ours!"

"Wait a minute." Duncan gave her a stern look. It was entirely phony, but he was a good actor. "It isn't the nanny's place to bring pets into the household."

Maybe *that* would bring about some admission, Duncan thought.

No such luck. She simply swallowed what looked like hurt feelings and asked coolly, "Even the nanny who sleeps with the boss?"

"Yes. Sorry."

Now the woman and the cat looked at him, recognizing him for the villain he knew himself to be. Ariel's brown eyes condemned, and the cat's green eyes pleaded.

The animal hung limply in his arms, his dark coat beginning to fluff out a little as he dried. But it was flea-bitten and dull and there was a ragged little triangular notch in his right ear.

He stretched up to kiss the underside of Duncan's chin.

Duncan held his gaze, recognizing another scene-stealer.

"What if I take him with me when I go?" Ariel asked, lifting the cat out of his arms and laying it over her shoulder like one of the twins. The purr was instantaneous and astonishingly loud.

It was safe to answer that one. "All right," he relented, knowing he wasn't letting her go anywhere.

She looked surprised by his capitulation. "Really?"

"Really." He went to the refrigerator, looking for something to give the cat to eat, and found one piece of leftover chicken.

He cut off a bite and handed it to Ariel to give to the cat, while he pulled the rest of it off the bone.

Ariel put it on a saucer on the floor and placed the cat in front of it. He sniffed cautiously, then seemed to consume the piece without even chewing.

While Duncan tore the rest of the chicken into small pieces, the cat climbed his leg, meowing.

Ariel laughed hysterically as he pried the cat off, and put the food on the saucer. The cat ripped into it with gusto, still purring loudly.

"I have the perfect name for him," Duncan said, wiping his hands.

"What's that?" she asked, still laughing.

"John Robie," he replied.

Her laughter stopped instantly, as though someone had flipped a switch. Her eyes widened and she seemed to gulp in a breath.

"Why?" she asked on a whisper.

Completely baffled by her reaction, Duncan thought back on what he'd said. John Robie was the main character in the Cary Grant movie he'd watched that morning—a character plagued by his past as a cat burglar when someone assuming his style began stealing jewels on the Riviera.

He couldn't imagine why that should upset her.

"You know the movie?" he asked.

She nodded.

"Well—" he pointed to the cat "—he was always referred to as John Robie, The Cat."

"Ah," she said feebly, "I get it." She forced a smile, but it wasn't convincing.

What in the hell, he wondered, was she hiding?

Chapter Ten

John Robie loved Olivia's skirt and enjoyed sitting beside Ariel on the sofa while she beaded. He would swipe at the needle as she worked it into the fabric, swipe at the beads as she strung them on the needle, and, when she wouldn't let him sit in the middle of the fabric for a better view, he would climb up the back of the sofa and drape himself over her shoulder instead.

His interest made it necessary for Ariel to keep the project in a plastic bag and open the top only far enough to pull up the area of fabric she worked on.

John was also fascinated by the babies. He sniffed them, rubbed on them, tried to clean them, curled up beside them when they were propped up against pillows on the sofa. He elicited wide-eyed looks of delight from them, but when their little limbs waved in excitement, he kept a safe distance.

He followed Duncan around the yard, perching on the finished part of the fence while Duncan worked on the last side. They had a different relationship from the one the cat enjoyed with Ariel, who held him and stroked him and gave him bites of meat out of her sandwich.

Duncan seemed not to notice him, but every once in a while he would stop to wipe his brow or sip from his glass of iced tea, then reach out to stroke John between the ears. The cat would close his eyes, lift his head into Duncan's touch, and purr his good fortune in finding this welcoming home with all its interesting people and projects.

Ariel watched one such moment from the kitchen window and prayed that she was going to be able to keep this relationship together.

Then the series of phone calls began that shattered the peace and set her entire world tottering on the needle-point of disaster.

Harper called on a Friday. "How's Olivia's dress?" she demanded without preamble.

"It's fine," Ariel replied. "I've been taking good care of it. I'm beading the skirt to match the bodice."

Harper oohed her approval. "I can't wait to see it. I'm supposed to warn you and Duncan that we're all converging on the summerhouse in about a week. Even Dori will make it. She's stopping in New York to take in my aunts' performance and do some shopping, then she's heading home."

Ariel smiled at the thought of seeing all of Duncan's family again, and particularly Dori, who'd come through for her so many times and in so many ways.

The timing of the family visit wasn't necessarily wonderful; she expected to hear from Cisco any day. Once that was settled, she'd be free to make a deal for her father, then tell Duncan everything—and none of that could be done while the family was around.

She could only hope that it would all happen after they'd left.

"And guess what else?" Harper asked, her voice edged with excitement. "I've saved the best for last."

"What?"

"Aunt Gracie heard from her friend in Canada. He sent the documents to her and she's going to give them to Dori."

Ariel's breath caught in her throat. "Proof...that Barton found Olivia?"

"Yes!" Harper shrieked. "A marriage license, *and* a birth certificate for Elliott Marbury Buckley!"

Ariel couldn't help it. She, too, shrieked into the phone. "I don't believe it!"

"I know. Isn't it wonderful? Skye's beside herself. She faxed Dori, and she said the four of us will have to convene in the attic with Olivia and toast her success."

"Absolutely. Oh, Harper, I'm so glad they found each other."

"It makes it easier to believe in happily-ever-after, doesn't it?"

Ariel thought of all that stood between her and that eventuality, then decided to take a step out in faith. "I've always believed in it. And two out of the four of us have achieved it. That's an excellent average so far."

She told the news to Duncan, freshly showered after a day spent finishing the fence. He held a baby in each arm and he accepted with equanimity the fact that his family was arriving en masse.

"There's no way to prepare for such an onslaught," he said, going to the sofa and settling into a corner with the twins. "So there's no point in worrying or trying to protect yourself against them. You just have to let them happen—like an earthquake or a tornado."

Ariel stood in the dining-room doorway, momentarily distracted by how comfortable he seemed to be with the babies, how he always scooped them up the moment he was free, eager to be with them.

"You're equating your family with natural disasters," she teased. "I'm going to tell your mom."

He grinned down at Michelle, who smiled back at him, then at Gabrielle, who swung at his face with a pudgy little arm. He leaned down to catch her tiny fingertips in his mouth.

"I'm sure their movements register on the Richter scale," he said after a moment. "And probably on Doppler radar. And it doesn't hurt to alert the state police and the Red Cross when they're on the move."

Ariel shook her head over his nonsense. "Do you mind leftovers for dinner? I'm afraid I spent more time beading Olivia's skirt than I should have."

"Actually, I've taken care of dinner," he said with a kind of royal finality in his voice. "Bertie offered to baby-sit for us."

Ariel raised an eyebrow. "When did you see her?"

"She came to kibitz with me when I was working in the yard. She was going to say hi to you, but she saw through the back-door window that you were on the phone."

"So...we're going out?"

He nodded. "Dinner and dancing. If you bring me their bottles, I can feed the girls while you're getting ready."

"Dancing?" she repeated in disbelief.

"Yes," he insisted. "I don't suppose you got much practice in the convent, but I once played a dance instructor/cad, so you don't have to worry about a thing."

"Really," she challenged, sensing something going on behind his seemingly affable mood. There was a subtle edge to it that she couldn't analyze. "And which are you going to be tonight? The dance instructor or the cad?"

He smiled. "I'm a two-for-one deal. Sort of like the twins."

"Lucky me."

WHILE BEING HELD in Duncan's arms, Ariel had a revelation. They were made for each other. It was as simple as that.

She'd felt it that night he'd made love to her in the little room above the cantina, and she'd dreamed it for the long year since then. But then lovemaking and dreams always heightened emotion and made the unlikely seem plausible, the impossible real.

But this *was* real. He held her so closely on the supper club's small dance floor that they moved to the music as one. The fit of their bodies was so perfect that they might have been poured together.

The edge that she'd sensed in him at home was gone, and he was all smiles and gentle teases and long, smoky looks across the table.

Everything in her responded to him, reached up for him like the lone tree inviting the lightning.

She felt as though the air sparked around her right now, as though warmth and wind brewed somewhere far above them and all the conditions converged to birth a storm.

She saw it churning in his eyes, heard it rumbling in his voice as he leaned toward her over their dessert wine.

"So, what now?" he asked, his eyes searching hers

as he caught her left hand in his right and entwined his fingers with hers.

She was mesmerized by the warmth and affection she saw there—afraid to identify it as love. She even tried to keep a small distance from it because she couldn't afford to give in to him now, to tell him everything and risk her father's future and her own.

But he made it difficult. Torturously difficult. His dark eyes moved over her face, feature by feature, so slowly and thoroughly that she swore she could feel their imprint. He played with her fingers. He smiled. There were suggestions in his expression that undercut all her carefully made and fiercely held resolutions.

"Well." She swallowed, deliberately misunderstanding. "We go to the Fishers' and get the twins, then…"

He was shaking his head, his eyes scolding her for trying to pretend she didn't know what he meant. "I mean, from now on. What do we do?"

"Just…what we've been doing," she said, her voice barely there.

"But you said Dori was coming home."

It took her a moment to absorb what that meant. And then she couldn't believe that she hadn't realized it sooner. But she'd been worried about so many things, juggling so many erupting crises that she'd missed entirely the real importance of Dori's return.

Dori would take over again as nanny.

Ariel would be out of a job.

The summer fling would be over.

She came to sharp awareness with a start and looked into Duncan's eyes, wondering if he'd noticed.

But it was difficult to tell. He seemed to have his own agenda tonight, and she wasn't sure what it was.

She felt completely seduced by him, but that might just be what she wanted to feel.

With the shocking realization that her days at the summerhouse could be numbered, she knew also that if she had to leave, she couldn't do it without taking her babies. And if she did that, he'd chase her down and reclaim them. But would he reclaim *her* as his duke had done in their fanciful picnic on a hillside in Yorkshire?

She didn't think so. As she looked into his eyes at that moment, her mind created a list of times and ways she'd deceived him, and she felt as though she might collapse under the weight.

"Is it going to be hard for you to leave the twins?" he persisted. "Or will you just find another family and stay in the nanny business?"

Duncan knew he was being a monster. Even when the villain he created existed only on film, something clicked inside him when he knew he'd made him live.

This time the devil had a pulse. He could feel it in his own throat when Ariel's eyes darkened with pain.

"I have a terrible headache," she said in a frail voice, her hand going to her temple. "Would you mind if we left now?"

He hated himself all the way home. He'd been despicable, and the plan to finally jar the truth out of her hadn't even worked.

Still, he couldn't dredge up much sympathy for her. He couldn't imagine a secret that would mean more to him than being with his children, yet she seemed to have one that meant more to her than did the twins.

After watching her with them for weeks, he found that hard to believe and accept, but he had proof.

When they arrived home, he called Bertie to tell her

he was coming for the girls. She told him they were sleeping peacefully and suggested he leave them until morning.

In the bedroom, Ariel was curled up in a tight ball on her side of his bed, John Robie stretched out on her pillow, fitted over her head like a hat.

Duncan climbed in beside her, pulled her into the curve of his body, powerless to know what to do for her—or about her. He couldn't torture her anymore, and she clearly wasn't going to reveal anything on her own.

So he would have to wait until he knew what was going on, then decide whether to hold her—or murder her.

The cat crawled closer on his belly, purring. He slammed his head into Duncan's forehead, curved the rest of his body on the pillow atop Ariel's head, and went back to sleep.

THE SECOND PHONE CALL came Saturday morning. Duncan had gone to the Fishers' to get the twins, and Ariel was alone, making coffee.

She recognized instantly the quiet, hesitant voice. Cisco had been eluding the law since he was nine and always looked and spoke as though he was just a footstep away from a long-armed *federale*.

"I have the tape," he said. "Julietta, you will have to move quickly. Your father is in trouble."

"I know that, Cisco. I'm in trouble, too. I'm being followed."

"By whom? Can you describe him?"

"Small, dark, glasses."

"That is my man, *chica*. You are fine. But your father has new trouble!"

"What do you mean?"

"There is to be a benefit to fund a library garden in Sandy Gables, Florida." His voice was urgent and low, his *r*s rolling. "A socialite who was once married to a Kuwaiti emir is displaying her jewels at a gala at the Silver Parrot Hotel. Remember, we once—"

"I remember." Ariel saw the nature of the trouble. "And my father plans to come out of hiding and relieve her of the burden of them."

"Yes. And Suarez does as well."

"Well, tell Papa that."

"I have," Cisco groaned. "He is going anyway. He thinks it is time he and Suarez had it out. You must stop him, Julietta. Only you can do this. I will bring you the tape tomorrow. You will meet me at the Buckley Arms at 9:00 in the morning in the coffee bar."

Ariel knew that the task he had set her was monumental, probably even impossible, but he'd been a good friend after all.

"I love you, Cisco," she said.

"I love you, too, *chica.*"

Ariel hung up the phone, terrified of the great burden—but with her heart bursting with hope. Proof! She had proof! This would be the beginning of the end for Suarez, and a new beginning for her father!

Just what it would mean for her, she couldn't be sure.

She turned away from the phone, a smile on her face she couldn't control, and saw Duncan standing in the doorway, an infant carrier in each hand.

He raised an eyebrow. "I love you, Cisco?" He repeated her declaration as a question. "Who's Cisco?"

He was jealous. She liked that. And she liked hav-

ing the opportunity to repay him for the taunting re-
marks about her having to leave when Dori came
home—whether he meant them or not.

She went to take one of the carriers from him, smiling broadly at Michelle. She took her out of the carrier
and put her in the playpen on the kitchen floor. "My
life didn't start when I came to work for you, you
know," she said with a careless look at him, as she
claimed Gabrielle and put her, too, in the playpen. "I
had friends before."

He leaned a shoulder in the doorway, conveying
barely suppressed annoyance. "I thought you were in
a convent before."

"Before that."

"When you spent time in Texas?"

She'd forgotten that she'd told him that. "Yes."
She went to the refrigerator to pull out eggs and milk,
afraid her story and her resolve to pay him back would
dissemble if she looked into his eyes. "How about
French toast for breakfast?"

"He's an old boyfriend?"

"Just an old friend. Bacon, too?"

"Please."

SHE DIDN'T WANT TO talk about it. Duncan had to tell
himself firmly that she didn't have to. In his efforts to
make her tell him what all this trickery was about, he'd
led her to believe that he had no lasting emotional hold
over her. That when Dori came home, Ariel was free
to go.

If that was her intention, he couldn't blame her for
making connections with old friends. She would un-
doubtedly need them.

But unless he was completely mistaken about her,
he couldn't imagine her walking away from him with-

out the twins. And if she was thinking that she was
going to set up household with his twins and another
man, she had another think coming.

Was that the only reason she'd found him again, he
wondered? To reclaim her babies?

He resolved to watch her like a hawk for any sign
of impending kidnap or flight.

When she told him the following morning that she
was out of beads and had one more pattern to finish
on Olivia's skirt, he smiled amenably and agreed to
stay with the twins.

The minute she was out of sight, however, he put
the babies in the van and went to town himself. He
spotted her car in the hotel parking lot. He pulled in
behind a pickup in the lot of the neighboring antiques
and collectibles shop, and watched the rear entrance
of the hotel.

An hour had passed and the babies were happily
gurgling in the back, the sounds of their rattles filling
the enclosed space. Duncan fumed, mentally listing
the things a woman could be doing in a hotel for more
than an hour.

Having coffee, his brain tried to tell him, and talking
to the woman Harper had met who also shared an interest in the Buckleys and Olivia.

Okay, those were two possibilities.

But the one that kept playing itself out in his mind
in vivid detail was far less innocent.

At least, until Ariel came out of the hotel a moment
later, arm in arm with the scrawniest old man Duncan
had ever seen. He was an inch shorter than Ariel, and
had a thick thatch of iron-gray hair and a lined and
wizened face the color of a redwood.

The man walked her to her car. She hugged him

fiercely, then hugged him again. He patted a small brown package that she held and apparently gave her instructions to which she listened intently, then nodded.

While they were still engrossed in conversation, Duncan backed out of his parking spot, completely confused. Choosing a direct route concealed by the pickup, he turned up the street at the end of the block and hurried home.

He was on the love seat with the twins in his lap, watching "Captain Kangaroo," when Ariel returned.

She stopped in the dining-room doorway to smile at him. "They're too young to appreciate that, you know," she said, pointing to the television.

"I'm not," he returned. "I like Mr. Green Jeans. How was town?"

She shrugged. Her hands were empty. He presumed she'd left the package—whatever it was—in her car. "The same," she said. "Nothing exciting to report."

"Where are the beads?" he asked.

Alarm registered in her eyes for just an instant, then she spread both arms in a helpless gesture. "They were out of them. They're reordering for me."

He pretended not to notice her apparent discomfort. "Good. We wouldn't want Olivia upset at you."

"Don't tease about Olivia," she said. "I told you Harper's aunt's friend found her marriage license and her baby's birth certificate."

"I know, I know." He raised a placating hand. "I guess I don't understand why you're working so hard on the skirt. I mean, the top's old, the bottom's new—it has no value to a museum like that, has it?"

"No, but she didn't give it to a museum. She gave it to us."

"Us?"

"The women who've lived here and cared for the twins."

"I see. Not us—the brothers who bought the place and have put up with you women who've lived here?"

She grinned at his dry expression. "You're unbelievers, every last one of you."

"Well, pardon us for trying to introduce logic into the situation."

"There are times," she said loftily, "when logic has no place. Is it time for a muffin break and coffee?"

"Yes," he said. "I'm due for a good break." If she noted the significance in his voice, she didn't react.

Chapter Eleven

The evening was warm and fragrant. Duncan and Ariel
sat in the backyard under the ash tree, the twins between them in the playpen, fast asleep.

With the pressure of her father's freedom and her
own future depending on Duncan's cooperation, Ariel
spoke as casually as she could. "I'd like a couple of
days off to take care of some family business. Would
you mind if I left tomorrow morning? I could be back
Wednesday night."

Silence greeted her question. She turned to Duncan,
who was slouched down in a lawn chair, his legs
stretched out before him and crossed at the ankles.

He turned to her slowly, his eyes in the waning light
clearly suspicious. "I thought you were out of touch
with your family."

Ariel stilled the impulse to shift uncomfortably.
Duncan knew she was up to something. She did her
best to maintain an innocent expression while sidestepping that remark.

"Will you be able to manage? I could ask Bertie if
she'll stand by to—"

"Where are you planning to go?"

It would be safer for him if he knew as little as possible. "I told you," she replied, "to take care—"

"I'm asking you where." he interrupted.

"It's personal," she replied firmly.

He sat up in the chair, angled one leg over the other and turned slightly to face her. His eyes had that same watchful darkness that now combined anger with suspicion.

"How does it relate to the man you met at the Buckley Arms?" he asked. "Are you intending to deliver that package he gave you to someone?"

It was as though the world exploded, as though the rubble of her life fell down around her in sharp shards, like the pickets of a fence, to imprison and isolate her.

She'd guessed Duncan was suspicious of her, but she'd had no idea he'd followed her to the hotel where she met Cisco. What else did he know?

She looked into his eyes, trying to read whether he knew who she was. But he wore that damnable look she'd grown familiar with lately that admitted his suspicions without revealing anything else.

She stiffened in her chair. Attack seemed to be her only course of action.

"You *followed* me?" she demanded.

"I did," he replied without remorse. "You lied to me."

"I said I was going to town."

"You said you were going for beads. Instead, you met someone at the hotel."

Anger billowed inside her. "But you didn't know I was lying *until* you followed me!"

He met her indignation with deadly calm. "Is that your defense?"

"I don't need a defense!" she snapped back. "I'm not the one who infringed upon *your* rights."

"Really." His manner remained cool and arrogant. "I thought my hiring you for a fair wage and benefits and entrusting my babies to you gave me the right to expect honesty from you."

She opened her mouth to refute the accusation that she'd been unfair, then realized she couldn't.

"I have never," she insisted finally, "behaved dishonestly with the twins—" she swallowed and added "—or with you."

He held her gaze as though to challenge her claim. She stared back.

He leaned an elbow on the back of his chair. "Then you don't consider it dishonest," he asked quietly, "to have a man's babies without telling him, abandon those babies to God knows what fate, hide from him for months, then invade his life pretending to be someone else?"

Her stare withered to a look of openmouthed disbelief. He knew…everything.

"You must have a considerably different moral standard from the rest of us," he went on, "Sister Fibster. Or does every convent have a nun who goes out into the world to tell lies and make hell real for us—to keep us on the straight and narrow. We Presbyterians, you know, don't understand how those things work."

She wanted desperately to scream and cry and explain that though she'd done what seemed to him to be terrible things, she'd always had his interests at heart.

But he looked as though he could watch her commit *hara kiri* without lifting a finger to stop her. So any emotional reaction to this sudden turn of events would have to take place privately, later and in the loneliness of her own room.

"I never was a nun," she admitted quietly.

"No kidding."

"I have my reasons for what I did."

"Selfishness?" he asked brutally.

She absorbed the insult. "At the time, I had very few options, and I chose the one I thought was best for everyone."

He reacted to that with the first real show of temper she'd seen in him. His eyes sparked and he got to his feet with a suddenness that made her jump.

"How could not telling me I had babies," he demanded, "and *abandoning* them, possibly have been best for everyone?"

"Dori knew," she said, her throat constricting with the desperate need to cry, "that Darrick would take care of them."

"Dori?" He jammed his hands in his pockets and frowned down at her. "How does Dori fit into this?"

"She's my friend. Everything she told you was true. We met while we were both students at UCLA."

"She's the one who told me you'd been a nun."

"That was my idea. I thought it would erase the last few years of my life, reduce speculation and explain away my plainness."

His angry eyes went to her short hair and her makeup-free face. "That did trick me," he admitted stiffly. "Angela Perez was very glamorous. So why the change?"

"I cut my hair when I went into hiding," she explained. "And did everything I could to look like someone else."

"Why?"

"Because I was *hiding*." She got to her feet and leaned into the playpen.

Duncan caught her arm and yanked her around. "Don't you *dare* get smart with me. I want answers."

Her eyes were enormous and reflected misery, but her voice remained calm. "All right. But we should get the babies inside. It's getting chilly." She pulled her arm from his grasp, picked up Gabrielle, and headed for the house.

Duncan scooped up Michelle, gave the playpen one well-placed kick of his toe to collapse it, and carried it inside. Michelle stirred against him but didn't waken.

He found Ariel in his room, putting Gabrielle down in the portable crib. He placed Michelle beside her twin and pulled a pink crocheted blanket over them.

He pointed Ariel to the hallway, pulled the door to his room almost closed, and followed her.

"It'd be best," she said with a formality that he felt sure was intended to keep him at a distance, "if you just let me do what I have to do. I'll explain everything when I come back."

He folded his arms. "No. I want an explanation now."

"I'm sorry." Ariel expelled a sigh, feeling bleak. "That's the way it has to be." She turned to walk into her room and close the door behind her.

But it wouldn't close. Duncan stood in the way.

"I'm afraid it isn't," he said. He followed her into the room, then pushed the door closed. "Everything's been your way until now. I think it's time power changed hands."

She stiffened her spine and met his angry gaze, refusing to be intimidated by the restless energy emanating from him. "This isn't about power, Duncan."

"Then what is it about, Ariel? Or shall I call you Angela?" The question was impatiently spoken as he leaned back against the door. "It's hard to identify the problem when I'm not even sure of your name."

"I said I would explain everything—"

"Later, I know," he interrupted. "And I said I want answers now. You were the one talking about rights a while ago. Well, I think I have the right to know the real name of the woman who made love with me and left me with twin girls."

She couldn't think of one argument, even a flimsy one, to offer against him. "Julie," she said finally. "My name is Julie."

She saw his eyes register surprise, then watched them darken. "But you worked on the set as Angela Perez. So…you were already hiding when I met you."

"Yes."

"Why were you hiding?"

"Duncan," she pleaded, "you won't understand without a lot of explanation that I don't have time for now!"

"Julie what?" He cut off the deflective answer he was apparently growing tired of hearing. "What's your last name?"

"I'll tell you—"

He caught her arm in steel-like fingers and she stopped abruptly. "What's your last name?" he repeated.

"It doesn't make any difference to anything." She tried to pull against him but found it painful.

"Then it should be easy for you to tell me."

She gave him a thin smile as she stood still in his

grip. "Certainly you've caught the drift," she said, "that nothing about this is easy. Duncan, you're hurting me."

He saw deep down grimness in her eyes that touched his conscience just a little, but couldn't quite generate sympathy.

He freed her by giving her a backward push onto the bed. She landed on her elbows, and he sat in the small chair that faced the bed, watching dispassionately as she pushed herself upright.

"After what you've done," he said, "I could get sole custody of the twins and you would never see them again."

The possibility of losing her babies had been the horror that had rumbled in the background of her every waking moment since she'd discovered she was pregnant. His threat made her mouth go dry, her heart punch against her ribs, her breath come in strangling gasps.

"You wouldn't do that," she made herself say, trying to imbue the statement with conviction.

He stared back at her without expression. "I know how to be a villain, Ariel." He corrected himself with a smooth inclination of his head. "I'm sorry. I should say 'I know how to be a villain, *Julie.*'"

"You know how to...pretend to be one." She breathed with difficulty, and her voice came out raspy and irregular. "But you aren't one."

He shook his head. "Acting isn't about pretense. It's about *being* someone else in a particular situation for a limited amount of time. And if you don't give me some answers right now, I will be the victimized father for the court for as long as it takes me to get the babies from you."

She didn't believe that he could do it, but she didn't know if she dared take the chance.

"I'm their mother."

"You are," he conceded amiably. "And so far all that means is a phony name on the birth certificate, abandonment of the babies, disappearance..."

Ariel heard the delicate snap of her own endurance. It had been one thing to maintain wit and composure when she'd thought that at the end of it she would have her babies and—she had hoped—her man.

But to think she'd survived the hiding, the running, the loneliness, and the lies only to end up alone was more than she could bear.

She flew at Duncan in a rage of frustration and despair.

Duncan had hoped for a chink in the armor of duty, or loyalty, or cussed determination, or whatever it was that was keeping her silent. But he wasn't quite prepared for the emotional earthquake that tumbled the wall and sent her leaping at him.

He tried to relax so she wouldn't break a limb or a rib when she hit him, while still trying to keep them balanced in the spindly chair. He shifted his weight to prevent them from going backward and into the wall, but he couldn't stop their sideways pitch.

All he could do was tuck her head into his shoulder as the chair tottered, then spewed them onto the hardwood floor.

Duncan's shoulder hit with a solid thunk. Ariel/Julie landed atop him and took instant advantage of her position to rain blows on him.

"Don't you *dare* threaten me!" she screamed at him. "You didn't even know who I was that night!

You didn't even *care!* So don't delude yourself into
thinking you're the ideal daddy, because you're not!''

Blindly, he rolled them until he knelt astride her,
his hands manacling her wrists.

''I never walked away and left them!'' he shouted
back at her.

''I had a reason for doing that!''

''Then tell me what the hell it was!''

She looked uncertain for a moment, as though
weighing the pros and cons of explaining to him. Then
her face crumpled and she began to sob.

Duncan was sure that he was going to implode with
exasperation. He got to his feet, lifted her up with less
care than efficiency, and dropped her into the middle
of her bed. Then he closed the door on her, as though
that would somehow settle the matter, at least for now.

But it didn't, of course. Her deceit and her unwill-
ingness to explain were like a brick in his stomach as
he went downstairs, made a fresh pot of coffee, and
drank until it was gone.

By one a.m. he could have climbed the Empire State
Building from the outside—even if King Kong had
been waiting at the top.

The telephone rang. Phoebe, he guessed, was calling
to nag him again about the Spielberg project. She was
the last person he wanted to talk to at the moment, but
he decided as he picked up the phone that she was
probably the only person he knew who could compete
with his caffeine high.

''Dunk?'' It was Darrick's voice, and Duncan didn't
like the sound of it.

''Yeah. What's the matter?'' Duncan demanded.

''Dori's missing,'' Darrick said simply.

If Duncan could have reached him, he'd have

punched him for the brutality with which he delivered the news. Then he realized there really was no merciful way to pass on such information.

"Ariel..." He hesitated, remembering that wasn't her name. But his brother didn't know that. "Ariel just talked to Harper, who said Dori was stopping in New York to visit—"

"I know, but...now she's missing. She flew out of Halifax, was on the roster of the two p.m. flight to Kennedy. But Gracie and Edith called when she didn't show up. Her hotel says she never checked in."

The brick in Duncan's stomach now acquired a companion. "Maybe she changed her plans at the last minute. New York's a big city, maybe—"

"Duncan!" Duncan knew that tone of voice: it meant shut up and listen. "Her bags are at the airport. She never claimed them."

Duncan said something obscene.

"Yeah," Darrick concurred. "My sentiments exactly. Look, we've got the police on it, but we thought it'd be better if we were all together. Mom and Dad are crazy with worry, so we're all moving in on you earlier than planned, all right?"

"Like you have to ask," Duncan said.

"And...Skye and Harper said that Dori's been helping your babies' mother. Seems there was a valid reason she left the babies. Only they don't know who she is. Only Dori knows."

"Not so." Duncan ran a weary hand over his face. "Now, I know, too. It's Ariel. Only her real name is Julie."

"What? The nanny? But why...?"

"I don't know that part," he said briefly. "Maybe it's something to do with why Dori's missing."

"According to Skye, Dori's been a sort of liaison between Ariel…Julie, I mean, and her father, who's a…" Darrick paused, then cleared his throat and said, "Are you ready for this?"

Duncan didn't feel ready for anything, but an older brother never admitted that. "Tell me."

"Her father's a cat burglar."

"What?"

"A cat burglar. Something happened involving a heist that went bad and everybody split up. And Julie's been in hiding because everybody's after her, from the man who ratted them out, to the police, to a cop who's a sort of Inspector Javert character, to her cousin who's been keeping tabs on her for her father."

Duncan was speechless. Of all the reasons he might have assigned to Ariel's…to Julie's strange behavior, having a father who was a cat burglar was not one of them.

Then he remembered the shocked look in her eyes when he'd suggested naming the cat after the burglar in *To Catch a Thief*. No wonder she'd reacted that way.

"Dunk?" Darrick prompted.

"Yeah, I'm here," Duncan replied. "How are the folks getting here?"

"Harper made reservations for them on the Internet. Skye's flying us and Dillon, Harper and Darian in. We're leaving in about half an hour. We should be at Foxglove an hour after that. Skye's going to drop us off, then go to Portland Airport to pick up Mom and Dad."

"Okay. I'll pick you up at Foxglove."

"Good. I gave the police the beach house number on the chance they come up with anything."

Duncan replaced the receiver in a kind of stupor. He hadn't had nearly enough caffeine to deal with this new development.

He turned around to find Ariel—God, would he ever adjust?—*Julie* sitting at the kitchen table in jeans and a yellow sweatshirt. Her face was ashen.

"I heard the phone," she said, her eyes large and wary. "Nothing good ever comes of calls in the middle of the night. What is it?"

Duncan's intelligence tried to see her in a new light in view of all he'd just heard. But his pride reminded him that she hadn't trusted him enough to tell him about herself. And his heart made him remember that she'd abandoned their babies—and him.

He took the kettle off the stove and filled it under the tap. "You're right about that," he said. "Dori's missing."

She started as though he'd swung at her. "What do you mean?" she asked after a moment, her voice small.

"I mean, we don't know where she is." He put the kettle on a burner and went back to sit across from her. He told her everything Darrick had told him, including what Skye and Harper had said. "Do you have any idea what could have happened? Has she been cat-burgled by your father?"

She stared at him one stricken moment, then went to the phone and stabbed out a number. She asked a question in Spanish that included the name Cisco—the name of the man she'd met at the Buckley Arms, Duncan recalled.

She was quiet a moment, expelled a gasp of distress, then fired another question, her voice rising an octave and gaining speed.

The answer apparently not to her liking, she fired another, angry question.

She cast an anxious glance at Duncan, said a very unconvincing *"Gracias,"* then hung up the phone. She resumed her chair, her eyes miserable with worry.

That did not improve his own nerves or his state of mind. "What?" he demanded.

"I think," she said, "that one of two things could have happened." Thinking about them seemed to require that she take another deep breath. "Sally could have her."

"Sally?"

"My cousin, Salvatore. He might have sensed danger and taken her at the airport."

Sensed danger. Duncan didn't like the sound of that, either, but it sounded a little James Bond-ish, even to a man accustomed to fiction.

"How could your cousin have sensed danger?"

"Sal keeps his eye on everything," she replied simply, confidently. "And he has the instincts of a panther. If a situation is about to go bad, he acts first to minimize the loss."

Loss. That was another word he didn't care to hear.

"Dori was probably just coming into the airport at the same time as Suarez, and Sally thought that had potential to be trouble if Suarez had any idea she was connected to me."

"But how would your cousin know about Dori's flight. And who the hell is Suarez?"

"She was in touch with my father on my behalf over the past few months, and Sally was her contact. I told you. He makes it his business to know everything. Besides—" she smiled thinly, not sure how

Duncan would take this news "—I think they have a sort of love-hate thing going."

Duncan had no idea how to deal with that information without causing a rise in his already-high blood pressure. So he asked instead, "And how did your cousin acquire this panther-like skill?"

Julie measured him with a look, then angled her chin and replied candidly, "At fourteen years old, he was one of the two best B & E artists in the eastern United States."

"Really. And who was the other?"

She expelled another breath. "I was," she said. "And he was only better because he was older."

For a moment after he'd heard those words, Duncan's brain was blank. It refused to function. Then, as though his programming had gone bad, all his brain would give him was profanity—a seemingly endless string of it.

He kept his mouth closed on it, and waited for it to stop. When it finally did, he managed to ask civilly, "And what's the second thing that could have happened?"

Her bottom lip quivered. He braced himself.

"Suarez has her." Before he had to phrase the question a second time, she explained, "The man who ratted on my father to get him arrested. Cisco—the man I met at the hotel—has a copy of a film of him shooting a policeman on a job my father was blamed for. I have to get it to the police and try to work a deal for my father. Suarez...might know I have the tape."

Duncan was having great difficulty believing that this was all real, yet his sister was missing and the mother of his babies had pulled off an elaborate hoax for some purpose.

"Why do you think that?"

A pleat formed between her eyebrows and she had to swallow to answer. "Because Cisco is missing, too. Since yesterday. Suarez had been laying low in the Caymans, but a charity gala involving a display of jewels is taking place on Friday in Sandy Gables and my father intends to be there with my brothers."

"Your brothers."

"Miguel and Eduardo." She swiped away a tear. "They're a couple of years younger than me."

Duncan was amazed that his brain continued to absorb ever more outrageous information. "When Darrick called, he told me that Skye and Harper told him that the mother of my babies belonged to a family of cat burglars. Of course, they don't know that's you, do they?"

"No, they don't." She shook her head and leaned urgently toward him across the table. "Cisco says Suarez will be there, too, and he and my father intend to have it out."

"Old enemies?" he asked.

She nodded, stretching a hand out to cover his. "Yes, and it's a long story, but Duncan, the important thing right now is that I *have* to go to Sandy Gables. I promise I won't be gone very long and I'll explain everything when I come back."

"You think you can stop the theft?"

She firmed her lips. "There's no one to warn my father but me. I have to try. And with the tape, I can at least clear him of shooting the guard."

The kettle whistled shrilly. Duncan made a pot of tea and glanced at the clock.

"The family's arriving in about an hour," he said, hooking his index finger in the handles of two mugs and hefting the teapot in the other hand. He sat across from her again. "I'm going to pick them up. While I'm gone, you will make reservations for us on the next flight to Miami."

She ignored the cup he pushed toward her, her eyes confused. "Us?"

He poured tea into the cup. "I don't like the idea of you walking alone into the middle of a crime where sworn enemies and the police are converging."

Julie thought that sounded decidedly protective and caught his glance as he looked up from pouring his own tea. "You don't?"

He met her eye without the slightest softening of his expression. "No, I don't," he replied. "When this is over, I want to be able to deal with you myself."

"THIS IS NOT going to work," Julie insisted quietly, as Duncan pushed her aside to toss a folded pair of pants and a T-shirt into the suitcase. The twins were asleep in their crib, and downstairs, Darrick, Dillon and Harper paced the living room, waiting for news of Dori. "If you come with me, everyone will recognize you and be all over us. How am I suppose to sneak around to find my father in a situation like that?"

He tossed in underwear and socks. "That won't happen," he replied, keeping his voice down. "Shades and a hat and no one will know I'm there."

"Like at Foxglove Field," she asked skeptically, "the day I arrived?"

"I wasn't trying to conceal my identity then. And get a move on. We've got to be out of here in fifteen minutes to catch the plane."

She stood directly in front of him when he tried to

put his shaving kit in the suitcase, and fixed him with her sternest look. "Duncan, listen to me. This isn't a movie. Suarez is a serious bad guy."

He leaned around her to toss his kit into the bag. "So am I."

"Will you listen!" she whispered harshly as she caught his upper arms and held him in front of her. She gauged by the flexed muscle under her fingers that he remained in place only because he wanted to. "Duncan, you have no clue what a real *evil* villain is made of!"

He leaned over her so that their noses almost touched. His eyes were dark with the anger he'd subdued to cope with his missing sister and Julie's crisis. "You're very wrong about that, Julie, and I am absolutely serious about this. And I'm going to prove it to you the first chance I get."

He slammed the lid closed on the bag and carried it to the door.

The telephone rang but he ignored it. He went to the crib to touch each little baby face and adjust their blanket.

Julie joined him, her eyes pooling with tears. "You should be staying here with them."

"And you shouldn't?"

"I have to see to my father."

"Then let's do it so it'll be over with."

They were halfway down the stairs, Duncan carrying the bag, when Darrick intercepted them. He handed Duncan the cordless phone. "Someone for you," he said under his voice.

Duncan took the phone and continued down the stairs. "Duncan McKeon," he said. He stopped at the bottom, turning abruptly to Darrick, meeting his waiting gaze. "If she's all right, then let me speak to her."

Julie ran the rest of the way down the steps. Dillon and Harper came from the sofa, faces anxious. David and Darian were curled up on the sofa, asleep, the Lab snuggled beside them.

"Dori!" Duncan smiled broadly. "Baby, are you okay?"

He listened, then nodded to everyone gathered around him. "I know. It's all right. It did scare us all to death, but Julie guessed what had happened." His expression altered subtly as he cast a condemning glance at Julie, then refocused his attention on his sister. "Yeah. Well, don't worry about her, just take care of you. I know most of it. Look, you just relax and stick by Julie's cousin. She seems to have great faith in his abilities. This'll be over soon. Right. I'll tell them. Bye."

Julie felt her composure slip dangerously as the brothers wrapped their arms around each other in relief. Harper forced her way into the middle, and Dillon and Darrick enfolded her.

Julie, exiled, stood on the outside of their communal hug and said her own private prayer of gratitude that Sally had gotten to Dori first.

"I really think you should bring us with you," Darrick said, following Duncan as he started for the door. "What if you need backup?"

"I'll be fine."

Dillon followed also. "You aren't *really* Titus Starchaser, intergalactic blockade runner, you know. You just do the voice for the Saturday morning cartoon. Let us tag along. If you don't need us, we'll stay out of the way."

"Oh, right." Duncan turned at the door with a grin. "Like the time you were supposed to stay out of the way when Darrick and I met the Ferreiras on the ball field and you pushed Binky Ferreira into the dugout before we'd even established the ground rules of the fight?"

Dillon grinned back. "He called you a yabo. And I didn't know then that you *were* a yabo, so I hit him."

Duncan put a hand to his shoulder. "And I appreciated your loyalty, but Julie and I have to do this."

"All right," Darrick said, "but remember that Mom and Dad will be nuts until we hear from you."

Harper wrapped Julie in a hug. "Please be careful. We'll take good care of the babies, so don't worry."

Grateful for that offer of friendship in light of all the trouble she'd caused, Julie hugged her fiercely in return. Then she followed Duncan into the early morning darkness.

SIX HOURS ON THE PLANE seemed interminable, particularly when Julie imagined her father walking into a trap of Suarez's making before she could get to him.

Duncan sat quietly beside her, somewhat like a guardian angel assigned to her—but not speaking to her.

They flew into Miami in mid-afternoon and took a cab to Sandy Gables, several miles northeast. The air was hot and sticky, a climate Julie remembered from her youth, and from her long period of hiding in Mexico. She closed her eyes and thought wistfully of breezy afternoons in the backyard at Dancer's Beach.

She heard Duncan groan quietly. "This reminds me of filming *Summer Lovers* in Manila in August."

She didn't open her eyes, afraid to lose the picture

of the summerhouse, afraid she was simply imagining that he was speaking to her. "Certainly you have enough money and clout now to turn down parts where you'll be uncomfortable—emotionally or physically."

He sighed. "Yeah, but before that I'd filmed *The Snowman Murders* in Bemidji, Minnesota, in February, so it seemed like a good idea at the time."

"I think it's one of those 'be careful what you wish for' things. Or maybe a 'grass is always greener' thing. Nothing's ever as wonderful as you think it's going to be."

From outside the cab came busy afternoon traffic noises. Inside, there was silence, except for the crackle of the cabbie's radio.

"Like that night in the cantina?" Duncan asked.

Julie opened her eyes, afraid *that* picture would form in her mind. She shifted in her seat to find Duncan leaning in the opposite corner, looking at her. He wore a white shirt and jeans, and the shades that had so far concealed his identity.

She remembered how wonderful he'd seemed to her in Mexico. He'd been warm and kind, and though he'd really had little to do with her, he'd always been the epitome of courtesy and chivalry when their paths had crossed.

She'd been fascinated, because when the cameras were rolling he was a conniving, cheating, drug-dealing border rat who used everyone to his advantage with lusty enjoyment and few regrets.

"No," she replied. "That was more wonderful than I'd imagined it would be—I mean my future in general. When I was a child, I was so sure I'd be a great lady with an influential husband and lots of children."

She took a tissue from her purse and dabbed at the perspiration on her brow. "But here I am. No husband, children I'm in danger of losing, and everyone else I hold dear about to go to jail. Not exactly my dreams come true." She folded the tissue and put it to her mouth as a sob threatened.

"I think," he said, offering her his handkerchief, "that we have to approach this with a more positive attitude."

She sniffed and drew a breath. "That's because you've never dealt with my father before."

The cabdriver pulled up in front of the Pretty Parrot.

Duncan caught her arm when she would have alighted. "I thought this was all going down at the *Silver* Parrot?" he whispered.

"It is," she replied softly. "This is part of the complex. The poor relatives stay here. This will give us the distance we need."

"Why?"

"You'll see. And when you register, ask for a corner room near the stairs. Tell them I have a fire phobia."

Duncan accomplished all she asked very smoothly, and registered them as Mr. and Mrs. Devlin Cross. She questioned him with a frown as they followed a bellman to the elevator.

"Think of it as part of your dream coming true," he said softly as he tucked her hand in his arm. "Devlin Cross is the 'influential' stockbroker of your dreams."

"Devlin who?" she whispered.

"Cross," he replied. "I played him on a soap. He was a selfish creep, but he *was* influential."

"But was he any good at second-story work?"

"He leapt out of second-story bedrooms when husbands came home. Does that count?"

"Madre de Dios," Julie groaned.

Chapter Twleve

Julie's head pounded as though she were the clapper in a very large bell. Her shoulders were tense, her stomach knotted, and her temper frayed.

This wasn't going to work. This would never work! What if her father suddenly came to his senses and didn't show up? What if he did come but she couldn't talk him out of the job? What if the police got to him before she did? What if Suarez did?

She sat in a bathtub filled with hot water and scented bubbles and wondered how the babies were. Did they think they'd been pawned off on someone else—again?

She tried to shake off that concern. Duncan's brothers and their wives had taken wonderful care of the twins before; they were certainly capable of doing so again. And Duncan's parents spoiled them unmercifully.

She felt a stab of emotional pain at the thought that she and Duncan and the twins might never be a family. She couldn't bear the thought of being without her babies, but she also hated the thought of them being without Duncan, or he without them.

He was a good father, and they responded to him so happily.

Abruptly she pushed the thought out of her mind. She couldn't deal with that problem and concentrate on saving her father from himself at the same time.

There was a light rap on the bathroom door, and Duncan entered the room carrying a room-service tray.

"What's that?" Julie asked, slinking into the suds self-consciously. When things were right between them, she was perfectly comfortable being naked in his presence, but his anger with her erased that comfort—probably because it was justified.

"Breakfast, lunch and dinner," he said, removing a starched linen napkin from the tray. "You haven't eaten anything since dinner last night. I don't think you should be climbing around rooftops while you're light-headed with hunger."

He carried a pedestal glass to the tub, tucking a spoon into the white stuff it contained before handing it to her.

"Is that oatmeal?" she asked, making a face. She sat up to accept the glass, forgetting her modesty.

"Rice pudding," he replied, either unaware of or ignoring her sudsy bosom. "Easily digested and lots of carbs." He put a china cup and saucer bearing the hotel logo on the broad side of the tub. An aromatic blend of tea wafted up and around her.

She looked longingly into the cup of pudding. "I want to eat it," she said, "but my stomach's in such a knot."

"Probably because it has nothing to work on. Take a bite and see if you don't feel better." He put the lid down on the toilet and sat on it with a cup of coffee.

"Have you called home?" she asked, dipping the

tip of the spoon into the pudding. "Are the twins all right?"

"They're fine. Skye got back with Mom and Dad at about 7 a.m. and, of course, they were all ecstatic to learn that Dori was all right. Now they're just worried about us."

"And well they should be." Julie swallowed the bite of pudding. She thought for a moment her stomach would reject the dessert. But once it recognized the substance as friendly, it seemed to relax. "*You've* never burgled before."

He sipped at his coffee. "True. But I have the other side of the caper mastered. I've swung across castle banquet rooms on draperies. I've walked the drainpipe on a roof, and I've escaped from an attic window by braiding sheets together."

Julie wasn't certain whether or not to smile. He sounded lighthearted, like the warm, amusing man with whom she'd conceived the twins, and the kind, witty employer he'd been before he'd suspected her of deception.

But he'd been doing that all day. He would forget his anger because the day required that they work together, but withdraw the moment she responded.

She decided not to chance it, and kept the smile to herself.

"Why are we waiting?" Duncan asked. "Why don't we just go to the police with the tape and let them protect your father from Suarez?"

"Because my father would hate me for interfering," she replied, "and I think he'd stand a better chance of doing less time if he turned himself in, and if he gave the police the tape."

"How did this tape come about anyway? I mean,

who tapes themselves in the act of doing something criminal?''

"Suarez. According to Cisco, he loves to show the tapes to his…hired ladies as a sort of…foreplay. That's why it took Cisco so long to get it. Suarez keeps them in his bedroom, and Cisco couldn't get at it until Suarez hid out in the Caymans.''

"And Suarez trusts these ladies not to rat on him?''

"They're probably afraid to.''

Duncan put his cup down on the rim of the tub. "Tell me about your father.'' He waggled his fingers in the water to check the temperature. "Tuck your feet in. I'll add some hot.''

She couldn't be certain that he'd be receptive to her efforts to share a smile or a laugh with him, but he seemed to be making every effort to see to her comfort, and she took that as a good sign. She might be being optimistic, but something was going to have to get her through this night.

"He was born in the Mezquital Valley in the state of Hidalgo in Mexico,'' she said. Half of her pudding consumed, she put it aside and picked up her tea, thinking how strange it was to be spinning out her life story to Duncan McKeon in a tub filled with bubbles. But then, her life had never been normal. "It's a very poor part of Mexico where the people had nothing. He and my mother's brother, Baldo, spent all their energy getting out, and went to Mexico City, eighty miles away, where they washed windows.'' She gave Duncan a small smile and shrugged. "You can probably imagine what happened next. They were working on a luxurious hotel, saw through the windows that wealthy people left expensive items hanging around, and helped themselves. They sent most of what they made back home, and kept the rest to keep the operation going.''

Duncan frowned. ''But weren't they the prime suspects? The scaffolding makes it pretty obvious.''

She nodded. ''They always did it after the window-washing job was finished, then moved on to another city. And they did different things—roofing, carpentry, painting and papering. Anything that would grant them access to rooms of the wealthy.''

Duncan looked disapproving. Julie understood; she disapproved, too. But she knew her father and understood what motivated him, so she felt compelled to add, ''He's built a small hospital in Madre Maria, a water system, a school, and they're now working to pave the roads and connect them with the highway so that they can get to the rural markets to sell the baskets and ropes they make from the maguey plant.''

Duncan absorbed that and nodded. ''Everybody loves a Robin Hood, but your father led you and your brothers into committing crime. I'm afraid he loses my sympathy there.''

She nodded. ''I know. Although I hardly remember her, I guess my mother wouldn't stand for the 'business.' But she died when I was six, and he went right back to it. He thinks he's doing noble work because that part of Mexico is simply ignored. The government doesn't care about it because it's mostly native and it produces nothing. And the charities don't operate there because it's so poor they can't even sustain themselves, much less help the people. So they get no help from outside. Except my father.''

''And your uncle?''

''He died five years ago.'' She swallowed the memory of the heartache they'd all shared when the man who'd always seemed more accountant than thief died of a sudden heart attack. "He was the one who planned things, and my father had the grace and the speed to carry out the plan. After Baldo's death, Suarez became the planner. Then he and my father had a big falling-out when Suarez wanted to keep the money rather than send it home. So Suarez started his own team."

Duncan appeared confused. "But why would he hold a grudge against your father when he now had his own operation going and *could* keep all the money he made from it?"

Julie put her cup down, her smile rueful. "Because every job he planned, my father got to first. He knew Suarez well from having worked with him all those years, and he second-guessed him very effectively. So Suarez planned the New Orleans job, knowing my father would get wind of it and do it first. Suarez had alerted the police and they were waiting."

"And you were involved in that?"

"No," she denied quickly. "I'd left the 'business'—as my father likes to call it—when I got a scholarship to college. He wanted me back for the New Orleans job because he intended to gain entrance through a little oculus window that he couldn't get through." When he looked puzzled, she added briefly, "It's a little round window. But I refused, we had a big fight, and..." She swallowed, remembering the bitterness of the argument and her own frustration at having her father's crimes a perpetual pall over her life. "I even said something about someday revealing him to the police so he'd be forced to retire. Then...the police were there."

"And he thought you did it?"

"I'm sure he did. Suarez would have been the logical one to have done it, except that then he'd have to admit how he knew and that would have destroyed his own operation. That was why I couldn't even believe he'd done it at first. He and my father had been friends for so long, but apparently greed outdistanced the friendship. So he bought off a cop who passed on the plans and its details as though he'd gotten it from one of his informants."

"Okay, two questions," Duncan said, putting his cup aside and leaning forward, his elbows on his knees. "First, why did you hide if you had nothing to do with it?"

She spread both hands, and suds flew. "Because the police were after me to find my father, and despite what I'd said, I couldn't do that to him. Anyway, I called Dori, asking her if I could stay with her for a while. She found me the job on your film's crew."

Duncan straightened. "And that's where I came in."

"Yes." Her air was suddenly blocked by a sob. It was noisy in the small room and she put a sudsy hand up to cover it. "Meeting you was...like letting light into a dungeon."

His expression softened just a little and he asked on a note of frustration, "Why did it never occur to you to tell me? Especially after the night we made love?"

A tear spilled over and she quickly wiped it away. "You didn't even remember that it was *me*," she whispered.

"Julie—" he moved to sit on the edge of the tub and pulled her face to his chest "—I'd had medication and a couple of champagnes. I remembered the lovemaking. I *dreamed* of the lovemaking. I just couldn't put a face to it because of my condition.''

She wept against him for a moment, then drew away. He handed her a towel that she held to her face. Then she sniffed and pulled herself together.

"I knew the condition you were in," she admitted. "I guess I even took advantage of it because you were talking about your brother Donovan and how hard it had been on all of you to lose him, and how responsible you felt about it. How it made you feel like a...villain."

She looked into Duncan's eyes and he saw an empathy there that it took him a moment to understand.

"I related completely," she explained, her eyes filling again. "I'd been a criminal most of my life, and even when I was trying to live a normal life, my father's activities were always like a cloud over me. It wasn't really that I was ashamed of him, because his intention was to do good. But I was always in terror that he was going to fall, or go to prison, or get shot. So...I knew what it was like to feel like a villain." She sniffed again and shook her head. "But you'd always been so kind to me. And when that actor was being such a jerk, you defended me and I *knew* you were a hero, not a villain. I just had to show you that. Only..." She shrugged her naked shoulders at the tricks of fate. "You didn't remember."

He leaned down to kiss the top of her head. "I did remember. I just didn't know your name." He raised his head to smile at her in amused affection. "Which was a good thing, because since then you've had a couple of them."

She laughed despite herself. "What's the second question?"

"Right." He helped her to her feet and wrapped her in the towel. "How do we find your father?"

"We wait on top of the Silver Parrot."

He blinked, then grinned. "You're kidding."

"I'm not," she said seriously. "After one a.m., when the party's over and everyone's settled down for the night. Duncan, maybe you should wait here. I'll—"

"No way." He rubbed her shoulders dry with another towel and buffed at the short ends of her hair. "I'm not letting you out of my sight."

She turned to him with a censuring frown. "I've told you everything."

"You have," he agreed. "But you have a way of disappearing on me."

"You have Michelle and Gabrielle. I'd never leave them again."

"Speaking of which…" He pulled a fluffy white hotel robe off the hook on the back of the bathroom door and helped her into it. Then he yanked off her wet towel and led her into the bedroom. "Why did you go to the hospital in Edenfield to have the babies? Then, why did you leave them?"

She sat at the foot of the bed. He sat beside her, angling to face her.

"Because you were out of touch somewhere in Africa," she said, her eyes reflecting the lost look she must have felt then. "I didn't know how to reach you, so I called Dori in England to see if she knew how to get in touch. She didn't, but she suggested I have the babies in Edenfield because Darrick was there. So she came to meet me."

He nodded. That made sense.

"And the D.K. McKeon on the birth certificate—"

she smiled wryly "—that was just an accident that worked to my advantage. Everyone on the set called you D.K., or Deke, so when I was putting your name down in my emotional, even overwrought state, that's what I wrote." She paused for breath, wrapping the robe more tightly around her.

"Then, I was taking a walk down the hospital corridor the day after I delivered and I heard one of the police officers in the ER talking to another about the unmarked car hiding in the trees across the road. They speculated over who or what they could be waiting for." She shrugged. "I knew it had to be me. Then as I walked back to my room I caught a glimpse of my father and Sal coming through the front door, so I ran, knowing that if they stayed to see me, the police would be on them."

"Your father escaped?"

"Sally must have gotten him away. He's been taking care of all of us for years. Dori hid me, then told me not to worry, that she'd keep an eye on the babies. When she went back to the hospital to check on them, your brother Darrick was back and she realized that everyone thought *he* was the D.K. McKeon on the birth certificate. And she suddenly saw that as a way to keep the twins safe and cared for while I was in hiding, and until you came home. After Darrick took the babies, she showed up at his place as though she'd just come home from Oxford, and hired on as nanny."

"But she could have explained to Darrick."

"No." Julie shook her head urgently. "Dori told me that all of you are into 'handling' things, and I was afraid he'd try to find me or my father to solve the problem and only end up getting himself in danger, or possibly ruining my cover, and lead Suarez or the police to us. I couldn't take that chance—particularly since he had the babies. I didn't want them touched by any part of this.''

Duncan could have objected that Darrick or Dillon would have been better equipped to deal with danger than she and Dori. But it was true that his brothers *would* have tried to solve the problem, and, considering the situation, that might have led to more problems.

God knew there were enough already.

"Insidious but effective," he said. "But my brothers got to love the babies. You're going to have some explaining to do to them."

"I know. And I know how much Skye and Harper came to love them, too. I never intended to complicate so many lives, I was just trying desperately to save my father's."

He couldn't take issue with that. "All right." He walked around the bed and pulled the coverlet back. "You'd better get some rest if we're going to be running around rooftops tonight."

She climbed into the bed as he closed the drapes, shutting out the late-afternoon sunlight.

She stretched a hand out to him from the depths of the bed. He came back to her and sat on the edge.

"Will you lay with me?" she asked. "I seem to sleep better when I'm curled up to you."

"In a little while." He squeezed her hand. "I have a few phone calls to make first. I'll go into the bathroom so I don't keep you awake."

"Are you going to do the King Arthur film?"

"I don't know."

"The girls and I think of you as a hero."

He kissed her knuckles and stood. "I appreciate that. Try to rest."

Julie watched him walk into the plush bathroom and push the door closed. Everything inside her felt cold. He was clearly distracted.

She turned onto her side, thinking with grim acceptance that that was hardly a surprise. He'd just learned not only that the mother of his babies had lied to him, but that she'd been a criminal and that she'd aided and abetted more criminals—his children's grandfather and uncles!

It was fairly certain her father was going to have to go to jail. But what would happen if *she* had to serve time?

God. The future—if she had one at all after she got back on the roofs tonight after so long away—loomed black and horrid.

She closed her eyes and prayed.

DUNCAN, TUCKING A black turtleneck into black pants, was doing something he'd sworn he'd never do…considering starting his own production company. This whole scenario would make an incredible script in which he could star himself—provided he lived to tell the tale.

Julie wore black tights and a black sweater and was busy tucking her hair into a black watch cap. She handed him a second one.

Beyond their window, the night was black, only a sliver of a moon visible. The main street was still gaily lit, but this little corner of town had quieted considerably: there was little automobile traffic and there were virtually no pedestrians. Everyone seemed to have settled down for the night.

Julie looked him over after he'd put the hat on and nodded, apparently approving his skulking style.

"Ready?" she asked.

"Don't we need rope and grappling hooks and traverse lines—stuff like that?"

She giggled. "You've been in too many movies."

"How do we get to the roof of the hotel?"

"These buildings are all connected."

"How do you know?"

She sighed. "I've worked here before. 1986, I think."

Duncan stifled a groan. "Okay, lead the way."

She did—peering cautiously out their door, then beckoning him to follow as she hurried through the exit door marked Stairs. She stepped over a chain hung across the stairway to prevent access, and raced up lightly to a squeaky door that let them out onto a roof.

A warm breeze hit Duncan in the face. He lost Julie in the darkness.

"Julie!" he called softly.

"Here!" she replied. "Ssh!"

He followed the sound of her voice, tripped over a vent, recovered, then found her when she turned to him, her pale face floating as though disembodied in the shadows. She was standing on the very edge of the building, and there was a four-foot gap between the edge of the roof and that of the next building.

"I thought you said they were all connected!" he exclaimed in a whisper.

"Well, more or less. Come on, it's easy. A running start is all you need. Watch me." She turned away from him, then ran past him and leapt.

His heart caught in his throat, but she turned to him

on the next roof with a "ta-da!" spread of her arms. "Come on!" she called quietly.

Wishing for the stunt double on his last film, Duncan walked a small distance away, then turned and ran, trying desperately to focus on the next rooftop rather than on the seven-story drop beneath him.

He landed lightly, and Julie caught his arm. "See?" she said, her voice cheerful. "That wasn't so bad. Only three more to go."

Duncan followed her intrepidly, finding it easier going when he pretended that a camera was following him. He thought of it as a second or third take, when he understood every move and every nuance required of his performance.

Julie finally brought him to a stop and pulled him down behind a sign where they could watch the door. "Now we wait," she whispered.

"This is the Silver Parrot?" Duncan asked.

She pointed to the peaked roof just opposite. "No, that is, but he'll have to get access here and use that fire ladder to get down to the room where the jewels will be stored in a safe for the night."

Duncan hunkered down beside her, his support pledged for the duration of this endeavor. But it seemed a lot depended upon what *should* happen, based on instinct and intuition, rather than on what *would* happen based on fact.

He prepared himself to help her deal with disappointment when neither her father nor Suarez showed up. Then he remembered that the redoubtable Sally must have thought something was about to happen, because he'd taken Dori at the airport. And scrawny old Cisco was missing.

Then Julie tensed beside him. He remained absolutely still and heard the faintest sound, like the turning of a knob.

Then the roof door opened. Duncan strained his eyes into the darkness to see three figures emerge.

Julie turned to him and pressed down on his shoulder. He took that to mean he was to stay put.

But he caught her arm instead and yanked her back. He ignored her annoyed glare and kept his grip on her, letting her know that if she was moving, he was going with her.

The three men, also dressed entirely in black, carried coiled ropes over their shoulders. They made preparations Duncan couldn't distinguish from behind. As Julie crept toward them, her foot connected with something in the shadows and made a light, metallic sound.

The three men turned. Julie stopped. Duncan took a protective stance beside her, thinking he'd be far more comfortable if he could see his opponents. But all that were visible to him were tall, slender but muscular bodies in black.

"Julietta?" the man in the middle said, forgetting to whisper. His voice reflected shock. Julie's father?

She ran to him and drew him down to his knees. The two men flanking him dropped also, and Duncan insinuated himself into their low huddle.

Julie and her father stared at each other for a moment. Then he crushed her to him, whispering words in Spanish that Duncan didn't understand. Then he held her at arm's length and shook her, his expression changing to anger.

Duncan clamped a hand on his wrist to stop him.

The two younger men moved to interfere, but Julie's father raised his free hand and turned to Duncan, the autocratic lines of his face in dramatic relief against the darkness.

"Who are you?" he asked imperiously. "You take dangerous liberties."

"I'm the father of Julie's children," Duncan replied in the same tone. "Take your hand off her. She's endured a lot to be here."

Julie groaned as the man's mouth went slack and his eyes flew back to her. The two young men he presumed were her brothers grinned at each other.

Duncan realized he'd unwittingly revealed something Julie's family hadn't known.

"Children?" the man gasped. "In the time you've been hiding from me you have married and had children?"

"No," Julie said with a sigh. "That is, we're not married."

That news did not please her father. He turned to Duncan, who was sure he was the next target for a shaking.

"It's a long story, which we'll explain when we get out of here. She's spent the last year of her life on the run to protect you, so don't blame her for any of this. She hasn't had time to get married."

The man looked very confused, then asked practically, "How is it that you have *children?* More than one. I saw Julie but a year ago and—"

"Twins," Duncan replied. "Girls. Do you really want your grandchildren to know their grandfather's a criminal, or that he's in jail? Please. Let's get out of here and talk about this."

"Papa," Julie pleaded, "the girls are so beautiful. Come with us—"

"Godinez! You're not going anywhere." Four more

men walked onto the roof. The stage, Duncan thought, was becoming very crowded.

"Oh, no!" Julie whispered in despair, as Duncan and her father turned to form a wall in front of her. She recognized Hoyt, the police detective who'd been after her father for years and, more recently, after her.

"Get out of here," Duncan whispered, giving her a push toward the shadows.

He turned quickly to block her visibility just as a dancing flashlight beam caught him in its snare. Julie saw that guns were drawn, and thought she recognized Suarez and Sally in handcuffs. Oh, God.

"Not a bad bag for us for one night, Frank." Hoyt's voice rang clearly across the rooftop. "We're tipped off by the notorious Dominguez, brains behind the Cat Pack, who leads us to Suarez."

"Salvatore!" Godinez cried, anger mingled with shock in his voice.

"Then we find the leader of the Cat Pack," the detective went on as though Godinez hadn't spoken, "his sons, and...who else have we got, Frankie?" Hoyt asked in a puzzled voice.

Duncan ripped his cap off. "You've got Duncan McKeon, detective. These gentlemen are helping me with my next role as a cat burglar."

"You don't say." Hoyt came up to him to peer into his face. "Now that's not what Mr. Suarez tells me."

"But Mr. Suarez is a thief," Duncan said lightly. "I thought you knew that, detective. In fact, I've acquired some interesting proof of his activities."

"Actually, Duncan, he's a burglar." Julie walked around him and handed Hoyt the film. "It's a small but important difference."

"Well, well. Julietta Godinez." Hoyt shined the

light over her. "Where've you been, young lady? I've spent a good part of the last year trying to find you."

"Securing this film for you, detective. It'll prove that Suarez's men—not my father—pulled the job where the guard was shot. The Cat Pack never carries weapons. And my family was just about to turn themselves in."

Hoyt scorned that suggestion with a look and handed the film to Frank. "And you," Hoyt asked Duncan scornfully, "joined the Cat Pack for the experience?"

Duncan smiled. "No, sir. I joined it for love. I presume since we've committed no crime, we're free to go?"

Hoyt laughed. "Guess again. We're all going to a cozy little place I know with bars on the windows, so that we can talk this all over and decide how long we can put you away."

Everyone was cuffed. Julie could not recall a moment in her life when she'd felt worse—except, perhaps, the day her mother died.

No, she decided. This was even worse than that. At home in Dancer's Beach she had two babies she might not see again for some time. And beside her was the man who'd never shown her anything but kindness and who she'd managed to get arrested and accused of burglary.

Then there was her father, who might not survive a long prison sentence; and her brothers, who should be going to college instead of to jail.

And her cousin. She looked up into Sal's eyes and knew that if he had led the police to her father, it was because he knew it was time to stop. He winked at her.

They were walked down the stairs to the hotel's top floor where they were piled into an elevator. Hoyt took her father and brothers in one car; Frank took her, Duncan, Suarez and Sally in another.

"Sal," Julie said, reaching up for his kiss on the cheek as he bent over her. Hands cuffed, they collided as the elevator moved. "Are you all right?"

"Always, cousin."

"Where's Dori?"

"She is well," he replied. "She is downstairs." He smiled at Duncan. "You are Dori's brother."

Duncan understood suddenly why Julie seemed to have such faith in her cousin. He had the dark good looks women admire, and the quiet presence that generated trust in other men. Even with his hands bound in front of him, he looked as though he could break free if he wanted to.

But Duncan concluded that he didn't want to. Considering he'd been quite a distance away only yesterday to take Dori to safety, he must have come here by choice.

"He's here to rat on your little gang," Frank said, seeming to enjoy the surprise and confusion on Julie's face.

"That's right," Sal said with a quick wink at Julie, as Frank looked up at the floor indicator. "I told them that I've always done all the work and your father always took all the credit."

Julie opened her mouth, probably to refute that statement, but Sal fixed her with a severe look. "You can't save me, *prima,* I've told them everything." He grinned devilishly. "A few years in jail will give me time to reread my Carlos Castaneda."

Julie turned to Duncan, her eyes reflecting her anguish. He saw her dilemma. Sal was doing the noble thing to try to save her father. She wanted to save him, but that would only hurt her father.

Duncan raised his looped arms over Julie's head and pulled her close. "It's going to be all right," he said, kissing her temple.

She leaned into him, tears streaming down her face. "Oh, Duncan. How can it possibly be all right?"

"Because I said so," he replied.

She sniffed and looked up at him, clearly stymied by his confidence. "Duncan, we're dealing with—"

He silenced her with a kiss on her lips. "I know what we're dealing with. Trust me. It's going to be all right."

The elevator doors parted at the hotel lobby. "All right, lovebirds," Frank said, taking Duncan by an arm. "Let's go. Let's go."

Duncan raised his arms to free Julie. In the middle of the brightly lit lobby with one sleepy bellman and one desk clerk sitting up to stare, Hoyt reconnected with Frank. Together they herded their captives toward the half-dozen uniformed policemen waiting at the double doors.

Dori stood in front of them, hands in the pockets of a denim jacket. She smiled. "Dunk! Julie!" Then she noticed the cuffs they wore and her expression changed to one of horror.

She went to Sal as they all drew closer, and her eyes melted with emotions Duncan found too complex to name. He thought he saw admiration, or even a touch of adoration, but it was all entangled with anger and a sort of resentment—but that didn't really make sense, so it had to be wrong.

She smacked Sal's arm even as her other hand reached gently toward him as though to caress him.

Sal had been smiling since the moment he'd appeared with the detectives on the roof, but now his expression changed—curiously—to reflect all the same paradoxical emotions visible in Dori's eyes.

He raised his cuffed wrists so that his hands cupped Dori's head and he leaned down to kiss her with a lust that would have sent Duncan to his little sister's defense if her hands hadn't been clinging to Sal's wrists, if her entire body hadn't been straining toward him.

"God, Ben," Frank said to Hoyt with a frown. "We got a whole mess of sex fiends on our hands here. That's enough, Dominguez."

Frank pulled Sal and Dori apart, and they were all loaded into a dark-blue van waiting at the curb.

Duncan felt a strange sense of exhilaration that seemed completely out of sync with the situation.

Julie leaned toward him in the van and whispered, "You're smiling! What's the matter with you?"

"I'm happy."

"You're going to jail!"

"I have a plan."

"What?"

"It's kind of an Arthurian thing."

She looked at him as though he were crazy. His smile widened as he realized that he probably was.

"Am I in love with a lunatic?" she finally asked, apparently deciding that she had no recourse but to smile, too.

"Why not?" he asked. "I am."

Chapter Thirteen

Julie paced an empty office in the Sandy Gables police station, while Dori sat in a chair, staring at nothing.

In the main office outside, it might have been midday rather than almost four a.m. Phones rang, various pieces of electronic equipment ticked, beeped, typed and performed other duties Julie could only guess at.

Hoyt and Frank had taken the men into another room.

"What could be taking so long?" Julie demanded of Dori.

Dori shook her head but said nothing.

"If Sally goes to jail, I'm going too!" Julie picked up the pace of her strides across the office, skirting a coatrack and a chair.

Dori looked up at her. "You have two babies to raise," she said. Her voice held no feeling; it sounded disconnected from her body.

"Duncan will do it marvelously. They can't hold him. He was there, but he isn't guilty of anything."

Dori tipped her head from side to side and rubbed her neck. "Neither are you."

"I eluded the police."

"Because you didn't want to squeal on your father.

Who could put you in jail for that? And your involvement with the gang was all when you were underage.''

"Hoyt could. He's wanted the Godinez family for a long time."

"Well, he seems to have most of them." Dori got to her feet and went to the window, rubbing her arms and looking out at the darkness. "How long will they get, do you think?"

Julie sank into the chair Dori had vacated. "I don't know. We've never been caught before. I suppose it depends on what the district attorney is willing to do. They've never used weapons and no one's ever been hurt during one of their thefts. They were even as careful as they could be to damage property as little as possible."

Dori leaned a shoulder against the wall and turned her face to Julie. "And all for a little village in Mexico."

"For their neighbors. For their neighbors' children."

"Sal said he spent a lot of time there. That every winter when your father went to Texas, he went home."

Julie nodded, then turned to face Dori. "You and Sal talked a lot, then?"

"Some."

"What do you think of him now that you've gotten to know him?"

Dori pushed herself upright and wandered toward the door. "That I wish I never had gotten to know him. That I could have just resented his interference in my life and his high-handed manner, and that would have been that."

"What happened instead?"

Dori yanked the door open and stood defiantly in the opening.

A uniformed officer who sat at a desk just outside said politely, "Need some coffee, ma'am?"

"No , officer," she replied. "I need my Jane Austen Compendium, my laptop, and my Harry and David's praline cheesecake."

There was a moment's silence, then he scraped his chair back. "I'll get you a cup of coffee."

Dori sighed. "Make it two, please."

"Yes, ma'am."

Dori closed the door. "What happened instead was that I found myself lusting after a criminal."

Julie smiled. "You're in love?"

"I hope not. I have too much work to do, and his criminal background isn't going to look good on my résumé."

"I know Sal, Dori. He'd look very good in your life. He's a wonderful man."

"He's despotic."

Julie laughed. "He's Mexican. He can't help it. It's an old tradition."

Dori frowned at her. "I grew up with three older brothers, Julie. I thought I was finally free of men watching over me, looking out for me!"

"When someone loves you, you're never free."

"That's what I'm saying. That's why I don't want any part of it."

Julie remembered how Dori had reached up for that kiss in the hotel lobby, and concluded she was part of it whether she wanted to be or not.

There was a light rap on the door. Dori pulled it open to admit the officer, who put two paper cups of coffee on the desk.

Suddenly Duncan appeared in the doorway.

Dori wrapped her arms around him. "Dunk! Are you okay? What's happening? Are they sending you up the river?"

He pushed her into the office and closed the door. He met Julie's gaze.

She stayed in the chair, sensing a certain distance in him, a kind of reserve she knew couldn't be erased until they'd had time to talk about where their lives were going now.

"No." He perched on the edge of the desk, moving the coffees aside. "I'm in the clear."

Julie leaned forward. "What's happening to my father and my brothers and Sally?"

"The D.A.'s working on it right now, but it might be a while. I thought I'd take you two back to the hotel."

Julie shook her head. "I'd rather wait."

"It could be hours. There are…details to verify."

"What kind of details?"

He shrugged. "I don't know. I'm an actor, not a cop."

"You've played a cop," Dori challenged.

"A bad one," he reminded her. "I did things illegally. That doesn't help me with this situation. At least, with the cop side of it."

There was another rap on the office door. Dori opened it again and the officer stood there, his face white, his eyes stunned. "Mr. McKeon?"

Duncan got to his feet.

The officer held up Duncan's cell phone. "You left your cell phone on my desk," he said, his voice sounding as though he were in a trance, "and you got a call." He frowned as he slowly offered the phone. "He says he's Steven Spielberg."

Julie vacated the chair and pulled Duncan into it so that he could take his phone call. She and Dori moved to the far corner of the small room to give him some privacy, but Julie listened carefully to his responses. He did a lot of listening, said "uh-huh" a few times and "that's very generous."

"You're welcome to stop at the beach on your way," he said finally. "My entire family's here, is the only problem. My mother will be calling you Stevie and force-feeding you potato salad." He listened, then laughed lightly. "All right. I'll see you in a couple of days."

Julie tried to imagine where she would be in a couple of days. Apparently she wouldn't be in jail. She was grateful for that, but she hated the knowledge that the entire last year of her life—and all the disruption it caused everyone—had been for nothing.

Her family was going to jail.

Another knock on the office door was followed by Hoyt's entry. He waved at them urgently. "Come on. I'm getting you out the freight elevator."

Duncan moved quickly, pushing Dori toward the door and hustling Julie to follow.

Julie resisted. "Where are we going? I want to see my father and—"

"Reporters are on the way up," Hoyt said. "If you don't want Duncan's face splashed all over the front page, we have to move now!"

Julie tried to push at Duncan. "Go," she said, then reached up to kiss him soundly. "I love you. But I have to see my—"

Duncan wrapped an arm around her waist and

pulled her firmly with him. "Don't argue with me right now," he insisted. "Just come with me."

"But—"

"Julie!"

She moved her feet, but the propulsion that got her to a rickety freight elevator was all Duncan's.

They were deposited in the underbelly of the building crowded with police cars and vans. In the middle of them, looking very out of place, was a sleek white limousine.

Hoyt opened the front door and gestured Duncan in, then bustled Dori and Julie into the back. The limo took off immediately, tipping Julie into the arms of another passenger.

"Papa!" she exclaimed in disbelief as her father laughed and wrapped his arms around her.

"Julietta." He kissed her cheek, then settled her beside him and handed her brother Miguel the other end of her seat belt.

"Mike!" she gasped.

He clicked her belt into place, then took her hand, his eyes dark and merry. "Hey, sis."

In the plush seat across from them, Eduardo rolled his eyes as Dori, who'd landed between him and Sal, stared into Sal's eyes.

Julie reached a hand across to him. He grasped it and squeezed.

"Where are we going?" she asked, her heart thudding, her voice high.

"To the airport," her father replied.

"To go where?"

He shrugged. "Home. I'm afraid you're going to have us on your hands for a few days. I cannot go home without seeing my granddaughters."

She stared at him. "Home," she said, certain she'd misunderstood and that someone would refute the claim instantly.

But everyone nodded.

"You mean you're all…free?" Again, she feared saying the word aloud, certain a voice from above would laugh and reclaim her family.

But her father nodded. "We are free, *chica*. Thanks to you and your *hombre*."

Julie tried to think that through. "You mean they freed you because of the tape? That clears you of shooting the guard, but what about all the other jobs? You've stolen millions, Papa."

Her father looked proud. She frowned at him. He shook off the smile and nodded. "Restitution has been made."

She stared at him, unable to believe that. "You've paid back four-million dollars?"

"*Si.*"

"And how did you do that?"

"We got…a loan."

The notion was too preposterous to be true. "Papa, why would someone lend the four of you four-million dollars?"

Sal grinned at her. "He said we had good collateral."

She rolled her eyes scornfully. "What collateral?"

"You," Sal replied.

JULIE, DUNCAN, DORI and Julie's family had been home since mid-afternoon, but Julie had yet to catch Duncan alone.

He'd shared a three-across seat with her brothers for the return flight, and they'd ridden home from Foxglove Field separately. Darrick's car had carried the men, and Dillon had driven Julie and Dori home in his truck.

Once home, Pandemonium reigned for hours. Everyone had been thrilled to meet Julie's family and to make room for them. Skye and Harper, who'd been holding the twins when Julie's father arrived, relinquished them to him. He sat in a chair for a long while, first staring at them in wonder, then playing with them as they began to respond to him.

Then Peg, her daughters-in-law and Dori prepared dinner. Afterwards, everyone gathered in the living room to hear the incredible story one more time.

Julie willingly accepted center stage on the ottoman to the chair in which Duncan sat, prepared to answer all questions, to explain all that remained nebulous, and to extend her apologies to everyone who'd taken care of the babies, as their own, in her absence.

"When I ran from the hospital, I didn't think," she told them, unable, even now, to believe it was over. "I didn't want my father caught, and I also didn't want the babies in danger. It all spun out as kind of a cruel hoax on all of you, but I never meant that to happen."

"All's well that ends well," Darrick said, Skye's arm around him, David playing with toy trucks at his feet.

Dillon sat in an overstuffed chair with Harper and Darian in his lap. "And it's ended beautifully. Or maybe I should say, it's begun beautifully."

"And I don't think you should take *all* the blame—" Darrick made a stern face at Dori, who occupied the other end of the sofa "—when it was our own sister who advised you not to confide in us."

Dori's cheeks were pink, but she held her head up.

"What's the first thing you'd have done if I'd told you the truth?"

"Scoured every inch of Africa until we'd found Duncan," Dillon replied, "and let him handle it."

She turned to Duncan. "And what's the first thing you'd have done?"

"Found Suarez," he answered instantly, "and eliminated him as a threat. Then—"

Diego shook his head. "He would not have been dispensed with as easily as that. He was a bad man, *hijo*."

Duncan grinned. "But so am I, Señor Godinez. I'm an acclaimed villain."

"Not anymore," Sal corrected. "Now you are a hero. You followed your woman into battle for her family. You saved the five of us from jail, and that allowed Cisco, the mole, to surface again. You are a hero, *hermano*."

The family loudly agreed.

Duncan was desperate to change the subject. He leaned forward to frown at Julie. "Where did you hide out," he asked, "after you had the babies and before you came here?"

Julie looked at Dori, who grinned and looked at her parents.

Duncan saw Darrick's eyes fly to them, then heard Dillon's muttered, "Don't tell me!"

Duncan looked into his parents' faces. Both smiled, no guilt visible.

"You?" he asked, caught between surprise that they'd do such a thing, and surprise that he hadn't realized they were involved.

"The babies were our grandchildren," his mother said defensively.

Dillon emitted a strangled sound as he turned to Dori. "And you weren't afraid of putting *them* in danger? You weren't afraid Mom would dig out this Suarez dude and set him straight?!"

"I made them promise," Dori answered righteously, "or I'd find another hiding place."

Darrick stared at his parents in stupefaction. "And you *agreed* to that?"

"We thought the babies would be good for you boys," Charlie said, putting a protective arm around his wife. "We all have baggage left over from Donovan, and all three of you had to learn your own basic goodness. Babies are great for that. And it kept it all in the family."

He smiled lovingly at his daughter. "I think Dori's the only one still struggling."

Dori pretended casual surprise, but Duncan had been reading her eyes since she first opened them. She was horrified at having been found out.

"I never knew Donovan," she said, her voice frail.

"And that haunts you. It makes you feel left out sometimes…disconnected."

Her chin quivered. Duncan saw Sal move from across the room, sit on the arm of the sofa near her, and take her hand. She closed her fingers over it gratefully.

"He was wonderful," she said, her voice strained. "I know I missed something important that everybody knows but me."

"Would it help," Charlie asked, "if I told you what a wonderful comfort you were to us when you came?"

"Yeah," she admitted, sniffing. "A little."

Dillon cleared his throat theatrically and leaned

around Harper. "You know, Dad. I'm pretty wonderful and important, too."

A loud groan rose from the group. Darrick whopped him with a pillow.

"You're only wonderful and important to you," Duncan told him. "And maybe to Harper, but she's a little shy of plum, too."

Harper laughed. "I thought that was required to be a McKeon."

David looked up from his trucks. "And a name with a 'D,'" he added.

There was a moment's silence, then Dillon put in quietly, "That's why we're thinking of naming the newest McKeon Danielle, to fit in with her brother Darian."

Bedlam followed the announcement. Everyone stood to hug and shake hands and squeal with excitement. Duncan wrapped his arms around Harper, then Dillon rescued Darian and moved aside as Darrick closed in.

Duncan turned to find Julie standing in front of him. She turned him around and gave him a gentle shove toward the dining room. "Okay, hero," she said. "Back porch. Now."

He resisted the shove and stopped just on the fringe of the group to threaten quietly, "I'd be very careful if I were you. You're a hairbreadth from ending up on the cutting-room floor."

Yesterday Julie might have believed that. Today she had a new confidence.

"You wouldn't do that," she said, hooking her arm in his and pulling him with her toward the kitchen. "I'm collateral on a four-million-dollar loan."

The night smelled of the ocean, the roses he'd just

put in, and the leftover aromas of good food and good brandy.

She sat down on the top step and drew him down beside her. She still held his arm and leaned her chin on his shoulder, her heart full and its beat accelerating now that she finally had him alone.

"I have such plans for us," she said, leaning forward to kiss his cheek. "I'm going to make you the happiest man alive, and our babies will be the brightest, sunniest children this world has ever seen."

"And which identity will you be using as you accomplish this?" he asked, apparently still not pleased with her. "That sounds like a French philosophy, and, as I recall, you once told me you were French." He looked into her eyes then, censure in his.

"No," she corrected gently. "You said the Bonneau name was French, and I simply agreed that it was. Because it is. It's just that I'm...not."

"You told me you were a nun."

"I explained that."

"You did. In fact you embellished it with all kinds of textured detail. Remember the cook who only fixed bland chicken and fish?"

"That was true," she insisted. "But she cooked for us in Texas rather than in a convent. I believe when we had the discussion, I wasn't specific about—"

He stopped her with a sudden turn in her direction. He didn't touch her, but she jumped anyway. He'd broken their physical contact, and at the moment that was a worse threat.

"I will not be lied to," he said, his eyes stormy in the light from the kitchen, "and then behave as though it's all forgotten after it's served your purpose."

"I explained—"

"You explained that you didn't want interference. Well, that's what husbands and lovers do. They're part of you—they're not outsiders expected to stand on the sidelines while you behave like some warrior woman. If that's the kind of husband you're expecting me to be, then think again."

There was a moment's silence. Julie, eyes glistening, swallowed. "That sounds like a hero talking, not a villain."

"This brief experience has taught me that it seems to take a hero to be a husband."

"So you've accepted that you are?"

"A husband?"

"A hero. Are you doing the Arthur thing after all?"

He leaned back against the baluster with a sigh of impatience. "Could we settle one thing at a time, please?"

"Sorry." She wanted desperately to touch him, but knew she had to bide her time. She smiled sheepishly. "What was the issue?"

He sighed. "Am I having this conversation by myself? What kind of husband do you want?"

She looked him in the eye, finally free of all her secrets. "I don't know. How many kinds can you be?"

That seemed to unsettle him for an instant, then he firmed his jaw and replied, "Just one kind. Usually understanding, generally patient, but with little tolerance for being tricked and lied to and left out of decisions."

"Duncan." She took his face in her hands and placed her cheek against his for a moment. Then she met his carefully unrevealing gaze. "The time in my life when I was most honest was the time I spent with you that night in the room above the cantina. Every choice I made after that, however ill-advised, was because I loved you, and the babies and my family. Please believe me.''

His expression finally softened, and she felt his hands at her waist. But his eyes remained serious. "I know that. I believe you. But I don't want you protecting me from anything. In my family, I'm the oldest. I'm used to making the decisions. *I* get in the way of whatever could hurt you.''

She was taking a chance here, but he wanted her to be honest. "Yes. So I've heard. But I'm going to be your wife, not your little sister, so you might have to make some adjustments in what you're used to.''

He raised an eyebrow. "And maybe you've been on your own too long and have to pull back a little on your Joan of Arc tendencies.''

Julie smiled. "She'd have been a great match for Arthur if we could fiddle with time and history.''

He rolled his eyes. "Please. We have enough trouble with us—and we're in the *same* time and place.''

Julie looped her arms around his neck. "I have no trouble with us. It's what I've prayed for and worked toward for a year. I love you, Duncan.''

The last shred of indignation he'd tried to maintain disintegrated under her admission. He cradled her in his arms and kissed her, thinking that she was finally his, but that she might always remain somewhat of a mystery.

"I love you, too, Julie,'' he whispered as he kissed her throat. "We'll get a license on Monday and get married before the family leaves.'' He raised his head to smile. "This house is having more weddings than a church.''

She sat up suddenly, concerned for him. "You're

probably broke now, aren't you? I mean four million…''

He shook his head before she'd even finished. ''No, I have a couple of times that. With a few major box-office hits and all I learned about stocks while playing Devlin Cross, I'm very solvent.''

''Darn,'' she teased, leaning her head on his shoulder. ''I was hoping you'd have to do Arthur for the money.''

He laughed and kissed her again. ''No. But I'll do it for you.''

Epilogue

Julie tried on Olivia's dress in the attic bedroom. Skye and Harper buttoned and smoothed, while Dori stood several feet away, waiting to pass judgment.

Outside, rain fell in buckets, thunder sounded as though the sky was breaking, and lightning lit up a leaden afternoon.

In the attic, happiness overflowed into laughter.

"I should have a backup dress," Julie insisted, as Skye fastened the last button at the back of the ruffled collar. "Just in case it doesn't look right on me."

"There's no time for a backup dress," Harper said as she fastened the silk skirt in place. "You're getting married tomorrow. Wade is sending my wedding hat by courier—even as we speak."

Skye and Harper stepped back to stand with Dori. Julie fluffed out the skirt and waited for their appraisal.

For one awful moment their startled expressions convinced her that she was going to be married in her jeans and a white shirt.

Then Skye said in a hushed tone, "You look... beautiful!"

"Like a dark Olivia!" Harper whispered.

Dori, eyes wide, gasped, "Oh, Julie!" Then she

turned to Skye and Harper. "Do you think we accomplished whatever it was Olivia wanted from us?"

Skye put an arm around Dori's shoulders, tipping her head to the side and smiling as she studied Julie. "I think she just wanted to give to us, not necessarily to *get* anything from us."

"But why us?"

"Because she was tied to this house," Harper said. "It's the last structure remaining that was built by the Buckley brothers and she apparently returned here as an old woman."

"But how would she have known what this dress would do for all of you? I mean, the house was bought by three men who didn't even know you existed."

"When the guys bought the house," Skye reminded her, "the bodice wasn't here."

"That's right." Harper pointed to her sister-in-law. "Skye was the first one to see it. Maybe Olivia detected something in Skye when she first walked in the door. You know what an impossible fix she had herself in at the time."

The women exchanged sympathetic nods. "Olivia had known great love for which she'd had to sacrifice and struggle. Maybe she just wanted Skye to find love, too. And then there was me and Julie. She probably got as involved in us as we were in her. Love has to make more love. Look at yourself, Julie."

Julie turned to catch her image in the mirror. The dress did look beautiful. The beads on the skirt didn't have the patina of age that glossed those on the bodice, but their pattern tied top to bottom, finishing the dress just as the dress seemed to finish the stories of the women in the room.

"The four musketeers," Skye said, putting a hand on Julie's shoulder, "have nothing on us."

Harper put a hand on Julie's other shoulder and reached out for Dori.

Dori tried to draw back. "No, not me! No life-altering love for..."

Dori's voice seemed suddenly far away as Julie caught sight of the other reflections in the mirror. Standing behind her were...Olivia? Barton?

She blinked, then looked again.

It was Olivia, dressed for the ball as she'd been in the photo. Behind her, a hand to her shoulder, a toddler in his arms, was Barton Buckley. Four older dark-haired children stood around them like satellites.

Julie was conscious of her brain working. India's children, it told her. Olivia had raised India and Barton's children.

Olivia blew Julie a kiss.

Julie stared, her heartbeats suffocating her, fear and fascination preventing her from moving forward—or backing away.

She didn't know why or how, but she had a window into infinity and she had to look. As she did, Olivia and her family shimmered, then faded away into a warm light.

Julie peered deeper. And then she saw her—a plump figure blooming out of the glow, with the warm smile she'd seen so often in the photo on the mantel of their Texas home.

"Mom?" she whispered, her voice breaking.

The figure lingered for just a moment, then backed away slowly as though waiting for someone to catch up.

A little boy in jeans, a NASA T-shirt, and a Mariners' baseball cap appeared in the mirror's frame.

Julie blinked, finding something familiar about him but unable to recognize him. Until Dori moved up beside her and gasped, "Donovan!"

The boy waved, then turned and hurried to catch up with Julie's mother. They walked away, hand in hand.

Julie took a step toward the mirror just as a crashing clap of thunder directly overhead was followed immediately by a blinding flash of light. The attic window shattered, wind blew in. Julie heard the screams of her companions as they were all driven to the floor. Leaves and debris flew in and around them.

The next thing she knew, strong hands were pulling her to her feet. She looked up into Duncan's anxious eyes, her own, she was sure, still reflecting all she'd just seen.

His fingertips went to her face, then scanned her body for injury. "Are you all right?" he demanded. "What happened?"

She nodded as she began to tremble. Had she really seen what she thought she'd seen? Was that even possible?

She stopped wondering when she saw Skye, Harper and Dori stare at each other, then at her.

"Did you see her?" Skye asked, her voice high and raspy.

Darrick brushed the tumbled hair out of her face and held her close. "See who?"

"Olivia," Harper replied.

Dillon sat with her on the foot of the bed and rubbed her back. "There's no one here, Harper. Lightning struck, that's all. It broke the window."

"She isn't here now," Dori said, her voice low and

shaken. "But she *was* here. In the mirror. And... Donovan."

She pointed to the cheval glass, shattered and lying on its side. Beside it, the dress form lay charred.

Sal caught her hand when she would have touched the form. "It is smoking," he admonished gently. "It will burn you." He looked around at the room, whole except for the broken window and the debris that had blown in. "Lightning would have been more destructive. There would be fire."

"Donovan?" Darrick repeated doubtfully.

"Donovan." Dori repeated the name firmly, drawing a breath. "I guess he thought I should finally meet him."

Duncan exchanged a worried look with Darrick, then surveyed the room. He looked over the faces of the women and saw their initial fear turning to exhilaration. "Olivia has been dead for fifty or sixty years, ladies," he said. "She did not come here today."

But Julie wasn't listening.

He was annoyed at first, until he followed the line of her gaze and saw...a bridal veil. It was attached to what looked like a beaded headpiece, perched on an angled overhead beam.

He stared at it, a little chill running down his spine, playing on every vertebra.

Julie felt the truth click into place inside her. She had seen Olivia. She had seen her mother. She had seen Donovan.

"Then who brought the veil?" she asked.

Her sisters-in-law were laughing and crying simultaneously, as Duncan reached up and plucked it off the beam.

He looked at his male companions, who looked at

one another in consternation, unwilling to offer an opinion.

Duncan stared at it another moment, then offered it to Julie. For the first time, his eyes took in the dress she wore. "I presume this was left for you," he said.

Julie put it on and turned instinctively to the mirror, forgetting that it was shattered. She turned to Duncan and saw such love in his eyes that she knew why Olivia had broken the mirror and destroyed the form.

No one needed them anymore. The past was gone. Everyone in this room was going forward.

"What happened up there?" Charlie shouted from the second-floor hallway. "Is everyone all right?"

The brothers and Sal looked at one another and decided with a collective grin that there was no explaining what the women thought they saw.

"The girls are fine!" Duncan shouted down. "Just a broken window. We'll be right down."

"Thank goodness!" Peg called up. "Hurry it up. There's a berry cobbler coming out of the oven."

As everyone else went to the kitchen, Julie stopped in Duncan's room to remove the wedding dress and hang it carefully away. She stared at the little cap and veil, feeling privileged and blessed by it, and tucked it up on the shelf for tomorrow.

Then she turned to find Duncan leaning into the crib where he'd placed the twins. She pulled on a high-waisted cotton dress and went to join him. She tucked her hand in his arm and leaned her head against his shoulder, happiness so large inside her that she thought she might burst with it.

"I love you, Duncan," she said, dangling a hand into the crib to catch Gabrielle's flying fist, while Michelle chewed on Duncan's index finger. She raised her head to look into his eyes. "Thank you for understanding."

He lowered his head to kiss her. "What's to understand?" he asked quietly. "Everything you did was motivated by love, and so much love resulted from and for everyone who got involved with you."

Tears overflowed her eyes. "Thank you for buying my family's freedom."

He shook his head. "I was buying our future. I figured after all you put into protecting them, you wouldn't be able to be happy with the girls and me if your family was in jail." He grinned suddenly. "And I admire what they did. Not necessarily *how* they did it, but why."

She kissed him again emphatically. "Do you have any idea how long I've waited for this moment—the four of us together?"

He put his arm around her and held her close. "Well, here we are—a villain about to take a dangerous chance as a hero, a nanny who was really always a mother, a ballet star in the making, and a really young rookie pitcher for the Yankees."

She smiled up at him. "The Yankees? Really? I thought you didn't want her to get that far away."

Duncan kissed Julie and smiled out into the moonlight beyond the window. "*You* found your way home to me. I've got to have faith that they always will, too."

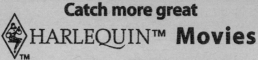

 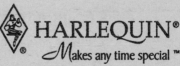

Mysterious, sexy, sizzling...

THE AUSTRALIANS

Stories of romance Australian-style, guaranteed to
fulfill that sense of adventure!

This November look for

Borrowed—One Bride

by **Trisha David**

Beth Lister is surprised when Kell Hallam kidnaps her on her
wedding day and takes her to his dusty ranch, Coolbuma. Just
who is Kell, and what is his mysterious plan? But Beth is even
more surprised when passion begins to rise between her and
her captor!

*The Wonder from Down Under: where spirited women win
the hearts of Australia's most independent men!*

Available November 1998
where books are sold.

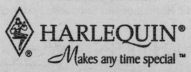

HARLEQUIN®
Makes any time special ™

SEXY, POWERFUL MEN NEED
EXTRAORDINARY WOMEN WHEN THEY'RE

Destined for Love

Take a walk on the wild side this October
when three bestselling authors weave wondrous stories
about heroines who use their extraspecial abilities to
achieve the magic and wonder of love!

HATFIELD AND McCOY
by HEATHER GRAHAM POZZESSERE

LIGHTNING STRIKES
by KATHLEEN KORBEL

MYSTERY LOVER
by ANNETTE BROADRICK

Available October 1998
wherever Harlequin and Silhouette books are sold.

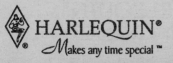

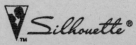

HARLEQUIN®
Makes any time special ™

Silhouette®